D1496022

# HReenee felt abundantly significant.

She was on a ship that had *killed!* A spacer that had destroyed dozens of spacecraft and slain thousands of Galactics.

She gazed at her hands. The single claw in each middle finger had extruded unconsciously. She studied them closely. Beautiful curved talons. She slashed playfully at the viewing port as if she were tearing out the guts of the spacers with her own hands.

She smiled.

# SPACEWAYS

# SPACEWAYS #17

## THE CARNADYNE HORDE
### JOHN CLEVE

BERKLEY BOOKS, NEW YORK

SPACEWAYS #17: THE CARNADYNE HORDE

A Berkley Book / published by arrangement with
the author

PRINTING HISTORY
Berkley edition / May 1984

ISBN: 0-425-06990-7

## SCARLET HILLS

Alas, fair ones, my time has come.
I must depart your lovely home—
Seek the bounds of this galaxy
To find what lies beyond.

(chorus)
Scarlet hills and amber skies,
Gentlebeings with loving eyes;
All these I leave to search for a dream
That will cure the wand'rer in me.

You say it must be glamorous
For those who travel out through space.
You know not the dark, endless night
Nor the solitude we face.

(reprise chorus)

I know not of my journey's end
Nor the time nor toll it will have me spend.
But I must see what I've never seen
And know what I've never known.

Scarlet hills and amber skies,
Gentlebeings with loving eyes;
All these I leave to search for a dream
That will cure the wand'rer in me.

—Ann Morris

We do not feel quite so powerless before a corrupt municipal police force as before a corrupt federal government (and military), simply because the scale of the former is not so overwhelming. How could we possibly confront the corruption and criminality of the state itself?

—Carl Oglesby

# 1

The bigger they are, the harder they hit you.
                                    —Sharjar of Bleak

She watched the destruction of the spacer in total silence. From the instant her ship, *Black Dawn,* appeared from no-where in the path of the freighter *Abraxis,* she spoke not a word.

Tura ak Saiping tossed her head impatiently to one side, throwing a glistening swirl of hair behind her. It whipped and curled like an ebony wave in the zero-G of her con-cabin. She had to concentrate on her actions without the distraction of that fine mane.

Long slender fingers tapped at the keyboard of her Ship Inboard Processing and Computing Unit (Modular). SI-PACUM responded instantly. Silently.

The moment she appeared in front of *Abraxis*'s prow, she ordered SIPACUM to launch three computer traumatizer lampreys at the freighter. The only sound the missiles made was a momentary hiss and *thunk* as they shot out of *Black Dawn*'s launching tubes.

Surprise was on her side. The freighter's Defense Sys-temry was slow in actuating—eight seconds from the mo-ment of sighting. In that time, she had already launched the lampreys and ordered her own DS lasers to blast the weapons nodes on the other ship.

She never bothered to confirm whether the ship was the one she wanted. She knew it would be, for Tura ak Saiping made it her business to know the movements of TGW freighters.

The DS gunner onboard spacer *Abraxis* managed to knock out two of the missiles closing in on his craft. He was a gunner in about the same sense that his captain "piloted" the ship—computers handled nearly everything onboard. The captain, the gunner, and everyone else merely turned the computers on and acted as emergency overrides.

Excruciatingly *slow* emergency overrides, compared to the computers.

The DS gunner, a round-faced young man who had never really wanted to be a spacefarer but who went where the money was good, watched in dismay and a fair amount of terror as the nameless spacer attacked without warning and immobilized his weapons. Then he felt a reverberation through the unipolymer plasteel deckplating.

"Impact!" he snapped into the inship comm. He said it with too much alarm, too much fear.

"Take us out of here," Captain Jarant Anstiss told his first mate.

One glance at SIPACUM's display revealed to that mate that escape was no longer possible.

"Fobbied, sir. They hit us with a lamprey. It's already gotten to SIPACUM."

"Comm the ship. Demand to know why we are being subjected to this unwarranted and—and *illegal* attack!"

"Comm is out too, sir. We can't transmit or receive!"

Captain Jarant, a short Ghanji who had allowed his hairline to recede under the mistaken impression that his crew would respect him because of his age, commed down to DS.

"Haven't you placidated it yet?"

After a pause and a crackle of gibberish from the traumatized comm network, a subdued voice replied, "We've *been placidated, Captain. DS won't respond.*"

"Prepare for tachyon conversion, then."

First Mate Jarant Kendis rubbed the bridge of his small, flat nose. "Sir, the lamprey has attached itself to our hull. It is busily fobbying our SIPACUM, our DS, and every other ship's 'puterlink."

As if in emphasis, the con-cabin's lights flickered twice, flared, and dimmed. In darkness relieved only by the confused flashing of the control panels, captain and mate regarded each other.

The captain looked with uncertainty toward the frantic, jumbled 'puter displays. "I think we—"

"It's blasting our airlocks!"

Kendis kicked over to the viewing port and floated close to the crysplas that separated the con from the vacuum a few sems—centimeters—away. With *Abraxis*'s telepresence cameras (routed, as was everything, through the spacer's computers) scrambled and disinformed and otherwise fouled up by the lamprey, human eyes were the only sensors to be trusted.

"Firm," Mate Jarant muttered. "It's wrecking them. We can't escape."

The captain joined him at the port. "And they can't get in."

"Don't be too sure, Father. Look!"

A hatch in the dorsal midsection of the attacking spacer opened quickly. Five spheres—the same grayish-blue hue as the plating of the nameless spacer—darted from the airlock.

"Cybers," Mate Jarant said.

Captain Jarant nodded. "It's the Dark Wolf!"

Jarant Kendis knew well of the mysterious pirate who plied the spaceways—identity unknown—attacking and looting freighters in flight. The faceless raider struck swiftly, accurately, and seldom left the target vessel spaceworthy. That the crew usually perished in the assault gave First Mate Jarant more worries than he could handle. He floated away from the viewing port and seized the comm-mike.

"Prepare to repel boarders!"

The ancient command reached less than half the ship.


Tura ak Saiping controlled the actions of her semi-autonomous cybers from the con of *Black Dawn* with a few commands tapped in on SIPACUM's keyboard. She eschewed vocally interactive computers, though she owned one for emergencies. Tura ak Saiping spoke little enough to Galactics. She had even less to say to machines.

The cyber-salvagers drifted past the useless DS nodes of *Abraxis* and waited a few hundred meters from one of the damaged airlocks.

"Krishna!" the DS gunner cried as a plasma bolt flared from the Dark Wolf's ship. It was the last word he uttered.

The blue-white blob of infernally hot ionized matter sizzled into the second hatch of the blasted airlock and melted through like a diamond drill against cheap plaster. Instantly, atmosphere punched outward. In a properly functioning ship, such a blowout would immediately be sensed by the computer and pressure seals would lock to protect as much of the ship as possible from damage.

The lamprey ensured that *Abraxis* functioned improperly at best.

Air howled out of the airlock, its staging area, and a dozen tunnels connected to it. The screams of the crew soon died in the airless void that carried no sound.

The gunner, wrenched from his chair by the force of the outrushing wind, reached out to grab a stanchion as he hurtled past. His fingers caught and held on. Almost as quickly as it had begun, the vacuum hurricane abated. The gunner floated in silence. Airless silence.

He heard sounds, though. In his few dying seconds, he heard his blood throbbing in his arteries, trying to burst through vessel walls and boil in the negligible pressure.

His lungs went first. Devoid of air, they contracted under the expanding pressure of his veins and fluid-filled organs. Other body parts tried to fill the void. His stomach and intestines swelled and burst. His heart seized up from the vapors of his boiling blood. By that time he was dead. A contorted rag doll that had been more boy than man.

Swollen, blood-filled eyes stared out into space. Eyes that no longer saw the cybers jetting in through the hole in the side of *Abraxis*.

Since stoppers would be no good against non-living matter, Captain Jarant and his son armed themselves with plasma beamers. They slipped on emergency breath masks. If the con-cabin lost pressure, the masks ensured that they would die in five minutes instead of one. The captain knew that— this time—every second of life mattered.

"Escape pod four is closest. Not badly damaged, either."

The first mate nodded and followed his father through the hatch into the ship's main corridor.

Tura ak Saiping watched the displays from each of the telepresences mounted on the cybers. One of them neared the main cargo hold. She watched it beam its plasmer at three floating figures. Two men and a woman scrambled for handholds in the tunnel, the gloves of their mobile life support systems clutching at anything handy.

The plasma beam seared through their mlss outer coverings. The resulting burst of relieved pressure masked the vaporization of flesh and bones.

That the boiling plasma continued through the three and punched a head-sized hole in the bulkhead beyond bothered Tura ak Saiping not a bit. She had no need for the spacer. Only for what it carried.

"This way," Jarant Anstiss said in a terrified hiss.

The pair drifted quietly down a corridor. Using the railing that bordered the bulkheads and deck, they propelled their weightless forms hand over hand. Since the relative directions of "up" and "down" varied depending on whether a spacer was under thrust, rotating for artificial G, or decelerating, the rails were on all sides. In zero-G, they provided a necessary means of locomotion.

Anstiss motioned to the younger man. They both stopped, ducking into the recess of a hatchway. One of the cybernetic attackers—"robot," they'd once been called—had made it into the pressurized area.

It rounded a bend in the tunnel and jetted past them. The hiss of its gas thrusters sounded like the whisper of demons.

From their hiding place, the Jarants saw the farrago of armatures encircling the grayish-blue sphere. Halfway between the equatorial ring of manipulators and the transceiver antenna at the axis rested a gleaming black TP camera. When it no longer pointed in their direction, the first mate let go a sigh.

Before it rounded the next bend in the tunnel, the cyber stopped dead in the air. Its TP detected motion. A crewmember rushed past the junction, panicking and groping for the rail.

The plasmer flared diamond-white.

A mass of charred and smoking flesh floated lazily in all directions from where the woman had been.

"Shiva's eyes," muttered the younger man. "Indrasta!"

"Too late for her. Go!" Captain Jarant kicked off the bulkhead and raced down the tunnel hand-over-hand.

Following him, the younger Jarant gazed in dull amazement at Indrasta's drifting remains. As silently as if they were already in vacuum, Anstiss overrode the computer control on the airlock and cycled the hatch manually. The pearly surface (marred and scratched by too many years of hauling cargo) slid aside.

The captain nodded inside. His brown eyes held the sorrow of crushed ideals. A captain never left his spacer. He knew that. He'd heard all the stories while growing up. He also knew that more often than not, captains elected to desert their ships. The reason was as old as the race called Galactics—where there was life, there dwelt hope. A dead man, no matter how honorable, seldom recouped his losses.

That did not make Captain Jarant Anstiss feel any better about abandoning his ship and what might be left of his crew.

"In!" he cried, kicking his son toward the lifeboat. He had heard the crackle of a plasma beam hitting cyprium. The dropping pressure had already set his ears pounding as he cycled the airlock shut.

"We've lost the main tunnels," he said, and nothing more.

The pair climbed into the escape pod and set the controls to manual. Jarant Kendis knew that the escape would be very nearly pointless. They were light-years away from an inhabited planet. The lifeboat possessed simple chemical and ion engines. He only hoped that the pirate—whoever it was—would leave *Abraxis* intact.

The lifeboat had its own computer, one that could operate independently of *Abraxis*'s traumatized systemry. The captain used the outside TP waldoes—large manipulators controlled manually from inside—to cycle the outer airlock. Nothing moved.

"Jammed," he muttered. "Blow the hatch."

The first mate threw a set of switches. Dull vibrations shook the lifeboat. Before them, the outer airlock hatch shuddered and flew away. Indigo space beckoned them beyond the portal. Relatively nearby, a hot B-type star was an eerie blue flare.

"Redshift!" Captain Jarant shouted. He punched in the thrust vector and took a deep breath.

The engines blazed into life, crushing the two men into the chairs. The airlock shot away from their view and they sped through the gem-scattered night of deep space. Twilight, really, here so close to star-crowded Galaxy center.

Onboard *Black Dawn,* SIPACUM registered the motion of two objects moving away from *Abraxis* at differing rates. One tumbled at a constant velocity while the other accelerated radially from the spacer. Automatically—and without the notice of Tura ak Saiping—the ventral plasma beamer flared into action. An actinic sphere of energy crossed the gap between the pirate's spacer and the escape pod in less than an instant. The lifeboat fragmented, the shards melting in the heat and condensing into soft spheres of unipolymer plasteel and cyprium.

Tura ak Saiping noticed the flash at the edge of her vision. Her only thought was a fleeting one—that the DS was functioning normally. She returned to her task.

The deaths of the father-and-son partnership called Jarant Pan-Spaceways passed unnoticed in the emptiness separating the stars. Only lawyers, a few months-standard from now, would really care whether the Jarants were dead or alive.

Tura ak Saiping scanned the spacer *Abraxis* with the aid of her cybers. No signs of life onboard.

*Good,* she mused. *One less crew of worms feeding TransGalactic Watch and its secret masters.*

She monitored the cybers in their progress through the labyrinthine passages of *Abraxis.* Sending three of the machines to the main cargo hold, she watched the telepresence screens display the goods available for her choosing.

The lights in the cargo hold suddenly flicked off. The temperature shot up. Tura directed one of the cybers to deactivate the ship's computers before the lamprey endangered the spacer and its equipment.

Once the computers were inoperative, *Abraxis*'s machinery returned to normal default functioning—lacking only a crew and a good portion of its atmosphere. Hatches still in working condition quietly sealed and the ship attempted to conduct repairs where possible. The lights returned to the cargo hold and the temperature returned to spacer normal of 22 degrees.*

One of the cyber-salvagers floated in front of a crate marked with the seal of TransGalactic Watch. A shipment of TDP anti-glitch devices. Source, the planet Sekhar.

Tura smiled. She'd been on Sekhar only a few months before and had been unable to procure one of the expensive, bureaucratically controlled components. The flaining bastard of a burok she'd bribed had taken the stells and *then* told her that TGW had backordered enough TDPs to ensure their absence from the market for almost half a year-ess.

She was pleased to discover that a portion of the shipment had found its way into her hands—or rather her waldoes. Four for her, the rest for quick and profitable sale. The cyber grasped the plascrate and maneuvered it out of the cargo hold. She ordered it to return to *Black Dawn* and gave her attention to the four remaining cybers.

One drifted through tunnels until it reached the late Captain Jarant's cabin. Unceremoniously cutting through the hatch, the salvager drifted about until its sensors detected the captain's safe. Carefully (under Tura ak Saiping's remote guidance), it drilled through the cyprium plating with its cutter, a molecular beamer.

An alarm wailed. The hatch behind the cyber tried vainly to seal shut so as to trap the thief. A spindly manipulator at the cyber's equator grappled on to the safe door and the sphere thrust backward.

Poison gas filled the room. The cyber didn't mind. It pulled the door free.

---

*Celsius—about 72 degrees *Fahrenheit*, Old Style.

Stopper beamers—set in the overhead—attempted to Fry the metal intruder. They succeeded only in warming its exterior. Damage, however, was likely if the cyber lingered in the captain's well-protected cabin. This it minded.

Tura knew what the safe held. She tapped a few commands into the computer. The cyber responded instantly.

Three precision sensors detected the sources of the sonic beams. Triangulating, they pointed the salvager's plasmers and triggered. The hidden stoppers vaporized, along with large sections of the overhead.

The cyber extended a waldo and seized the contents of the safe: a slim gray and maroon equhyde packet. Depositing it in an interior compartment, the cyber gymballed about and thrust toward the simplest path to *Black Dawn*—the cabin's wide viewing port.

The metal thief burned a neat hole in the crysplas with its plasmer. The outrush of what little atmosphere remained in the cabin (mostly an enzymatic poison gas called 3-4-3 Gamma Dioxylase) propelled the sphere through with an extra push. It retracted its farrago of arms and passed the fused edges of the port with room to spare.

The gray and maroon packet it carried contained twenty slim pieces of plastic. They looked unimpressive. Only the fact that they were sealed in a TGW Priority Transferral Pouch indicated their true value. Any Galactic banker would immediately identify them as negotiable credcassettes. Millions of stells worth. A droplet in TGW's operating budget (a month's payroll and expenses for TGW personnel and TGO AiP's on Terasaki and Franji), it represented a fortune in the hands of one person.

Tura ak Saiping was that person. She smiled coolly and concentrated on the remaining three salvagers. A thin film of perspiration glowed on her golden-bronze skin.

One of the cybers she sent back to her ship with a load

of quark-tunnel microcomputer components. They were being shipped to a TGW (and, presumably, TGO) research facility. She had the cyber rip open the sealed documents attached to the container. She frowned when she read what the cyber held up to its TP.

*Why would there be a TGW research station just a half light-year away from Shirash?*

Most Galactics shuddered at the mere mention of the planet that gave birth to a race of amorphous monstrosities possessing intensely powerful telehypnotic abilities. Tura ak Saiping merely continued to frown. As far as she knew, TGW maintained an uncrewed cybercraft in orbit around the watery world. It served as a warning buoy, alerting spacefarers to the almost unopposable danger below. That monitor would also alert TransGalactic Watch, *pres* meaning fast, if the jelly-blobs of Shirash ever escaped their planet and moved out along the spaceways.

*One less load of equipment for whatever they're "researching" near that abominable planet,* she mused in satisfaction. *Or anywhere else!*

The other cyber in the main cargo hold bypassed crates of food and drink-flavorings, farm machinery (although that was an ancient cover-phrase for weapons, ref: the Caribbean Connection), holotapes, uniforms, and mining equipment. Thousands and thousands of stells' worth of stuff, all doubtless urgently needed for something, by . . . someone. It was not the cybers' business, however, to consider the poor starving children of Fill-In-The-Blank. That was of no concern to their captain, either.

The cybernetic member of Tura ak Saiping's crew in the main cargo hold paused at a small crate marked with the TGW seal and the words 300 EACH: MULTIFUNCTIONAL PERSONAL BEAM-SIDEARM: SONIC.

Tura paused, too. She debated taking the crate of stoppers

onboard her spacer. *Enough stoppers there to arm a little army and start a revolution or rebellion at the very least,* she thought. Then she sneered at her own concept: *Sure. And be wiped out by TGO. No no, Tura, no one's doing that. If there were a revolutionary force somewhere, wouldn't you love to know about it!*

Again she answered her own thought to the contrary: *No. Tura's a loner, and a loner I'll stay.*

Still, all those stoppers would fetch a nice price. On the other hand, her *Black Dawn* was the smallest ship able to utilize tachyon-conversion systemry and still require a crew of only one. The Corsi-built Masoch Mark IV had no life-boats or landers for swooping down into gravity. Tura's ship was built for speed, stealth—for piracy.

It was not built for hauling freight. The two crates already on their way to *Black Dawn* would fill its hold. Reluctantly, Tura ordered the cyber to pass up the stoppers, despite the high demand for weapons all along the spaceways. She hoped to find something more valuable and less bulky.

The cyber found just that, a moment later.

A container the size of a go-bag lay strapped unpretentiously atop a shipper of Bleak's only beer, Puce Ribbon. Even though separated by hundreds of meters of vacuum, Tura reflexively wrinkled her nose. She thought of TransGalactic Watch personnel as scum, as policer scum of the lowest sort, but such bad taste in potables appalled her.

*Probably some subsidized export program that Bleak can't afford anyway. Maybe the whole damned planet'll go broke close down. No more Bleak!*

*Who'd notice?*

She tapped in a command for the cyber to scan the smaller container. She nodded, eyes narrowing. *Drugs.* Captured incidentally in some raid on a slaver or pirate or smuggler and being transported as evidence, for storage. Or perhaps to a disposal facility.

The cyber took it in one "hand" and flew out. Back to *Black Dawn*.

The last of her cybernetic crew floated to the center of the ship. It was not a salvager. Its function was not to take anything, but to leave something behind. Seeking the ship's center of mass with its delicate sensors, the cyber drifted along corridor-tunnels, always farther in.

When it could go no farther, it released a cubic object measuring a half-meter on a side. The cube drifted until it touched a bulkhead, where it lightly adhered. Just a large building block, gray and red.

The cyber wended its way out of *Abraxis*.

When Tura ak Saiping firmed that all five cybercrew-members were safely onboard and had stored away their loot, she moved *Black Dawn* out to a hundred kloms' distance and triggered the shockwave bomb left at the center of the freighter.

She watched the spacer's silent death in silence.

The hull of *Abraxis* burst at several junctures. Fuels and remaining atmosphere mushroomed out of the fractures, the debris expanding from the ship like the blossoming of a rose. For a moment, the entire ship quaked with interior shocks. Then something in the depths of the spacer flared to the surface.

*Abraxis* was shattered into a thousand pieces, as if struck interiorly with a thousand giant hammers.

She watched the bits of slag glow in hues from white to yellow to orange to dull red, while surrounding stars seemed to fade and vanish. She smiled with grim pleasure and felt the warmth between her lithe thighs grow to fiery levels. Slowly she rotated her hips, clamped and eased her thighs, to send the lovely sensations coursing through her.

*No survivors,* she thought, and her hands drifted over to squeeze her own breast, with force. *No lackey worms left alive!*

How delicious! How . . . erotic!

She tightened the straps of the master's chair (the only chair in the con-cabin) and rubbed against the seat even harder, squeezing her thighs together until they trembled with the delightful strain. In the null-G, her long black, black hair whipped about her wide shoulders. Her smile formed a cruel, blood-red slash between her wide lips.

Bits of slag end-over-ended about her, drifting, adding to the surprisingly great mass of matter that cluttered the so-called "void" of space. Abraxis *and its crew will not rest in peace,* she thought, *but drift forever in pieces.* The thought sent a new surge of welcome sensual delight all through her.

She inslotted a navigation cassette containing instructions to SIPACUM for the trip to her next destination—Mirjam—and a well-paying but undiscriminating dealer in unregistered goods. She swept her gaze over the glittering jewels of the freighter's demise, and she was feeling *good.*

*Death to you, TransGalactic Ordure! And your toadying freighters.*

Her long eyelids closed, their long lashes jet fans on her cheeks, barely fluttering beneath the narrow epicanthic folds . . . which Tura ak Saiping had added herself, along with her name. And along with her declaration of war on TGO and its uniformed arm, TGW. And its so-necessary freighters.

SIPACUM *ping*ged twice, indicating ninety seconds to tachyon conversion and faster-than-light travel.

Time enough. Her hand snaked down to her loins to finish what her destroying *Abraxis* had commenced.

# 2

Always and ever the government and its rulers and operators have been considered above the general moral law. . . . Service to the State is supposed to excuse all actions that would be considered immoral or criminal if committed by "private" citizens.

—Murray N. Rothbard, *For a New Liberty*

Marekallian Eks was ready to bash heads together.

The Outreacher sat in a conference chamber as austere and functional as a prison lunchroom. Throughout the green and beige enclosure squatted unimposing chairs and tables. Nearly a hundred people sat or stood, listening to the current speaker.

Marekallian Eks listened, too, with blatantly evident impatience. If there were any place else in the Galaxy he could have been, he would have been there rather than at this meeting of the Council of Ninety-Three. He would much rather have been engaging in his Mindrunning activities, bringing technology to the people of Protected planets, boosting their intelligence (and looting their temples).* Only his hatred of TGO brought Marekallian Eks to this alliance of financiers, smugglers, manufacturers and idealists; and kept him involved as its foremost activist.

The speaker—a banker from Samanna—droned on in a

---

*As in SPACEWAYS #13, *Jonuta Rising!*

gratingly nasal tone about the predacious behavior of TGW's "fee" collectors on his native planet.

"They are nothing more than gangsters, collecting their 'protection' money and strutting about in their little uniforms interfering with commerce, sticking their noses in—"

"Thank you, Prastiba-seety," Eks said to the Sam. "I think your view is quite obviously shared by the other members of the Council. That's why we're here." He stifled a yawn and continued. "This meeting is intended to be a strategy session on how best to use our resources. Resources such as *time, Myrzha* Prastiba."

Eks gazed around the chamber at the faces turned toward him. Human, mostly—that spacefaring race that called itself Galactic and seemed to be proving worthy of the name— plus a few Jarps and an actual Crozer, robed. The Crozers looked Galactic in all aspects, yet they differed on a genetic level that prevented cross-breeding. That made them something other than human. So did that unpleasant pineal eye.

A Jarp spoke up. The translation helmet it wore converted the whistles of its thin, long tongue into Erts, the language of the spaceways. It gestured with its slender orange arms and shook its heart-shaped head so that rich, burgundy-hued hair rippled and shimmered in the lights.

Eks ignored the words it spoke through its translahelm. He was thinking about a woman. A woman just a few months back and half a Galaxy away.

"You don't expect," she had said, "that we'll be able to get away with him *and* the loot?"

She strode along one of the tunnels near the surface of spacer *Coronet* and glanced from Marekallian to the Akil.

The downy-furred alien stared back at her with eyes the color of gold dust. He stood shorter than either she—Verley of Sekhar—or the man she addressed.

Eks ran a tanned set of fingers across his jet black hair down to where it ended in a queue.

"Oh," he said with a nonchalant air, "I think I'll be able to."

He put an arm around the white-gold furred shoulders of the Akil. The gentle-looking creature continued walking but stared up at him inquiringly with eyes larger than a Jarp's. It (he—the Akil was quite obviously male) could have evolved to its humanoid status from the lemurs of Homeworld—Urth. His long fingers reached up to grasp the Galactic's wrist. That grip was strong, belying the delicacy of his build.

Eks and Verley had seen the frail alien jump four meters up a wall with little more than a running start. From ankle-deep water. Only moments after being awakened from its cryosphere in a treasure vault on a distant Protected planet called Arepien.*

The Mindrunner, who had looted the vault as "payment" for making the surface-dwellers aware of Galactic civilization, now had to deal with a more formidable opponent. The captain of *Coronet*.

"Leave our host to me," he said, eyeing the lovely woman from Sekhar and patting the Akil's arm. He disengaged from the Akil upon reaching the con-cabin and signaled their presence.

"Enter," a deep basso voice boomed.

The con-cabin hatch slid open to admit the trio. At the con stood a man of 180 sems height. He wore linden-green equhyde tights and an imposing long-tailed coat of piratical scarlet. When he turned, a double row of brass-imitating prass buttons reflected glints of light from the flashing and flickering telits. The captain of spacer *Coronet* faced his "passengers."

---

*In *Jonuta Rising!*

Marek spoke up first. "I see you got the *kunda* vine sap off your clothes. Or do you stock identical outfits?"

Captain Kislar Jonuta of Qalara smiled.

"We are in orbit around Jasbir, Mindrunner. This is where I expect to pick up some, uh, cargo. And let you off."

"With Phoenix, slaver." Eks grinned with feral enjoyment. "Your thirty-five per cent of *my* recovery doesn't include sentient beings."

Jonuta smiled wanly. His coal-sack eyes glimmered with feigned menace. "I'll take—as my *forty* per cent for saving you from TGW—the Akil. Period. I won't even touch your loot."

*"Loot!* I was nearly killed removing those barbarous relics of Arepien's superstitions." He looked genuinely hurt— as genuine as he could improvise. "I've brainboosted enough of them that they'll be spacefarers in a few decades, if they exert themselves. They don't need their old gods now." The Outreacher slid an arm protectively around the Akil. "I insist that I keep Phoenix. I'm the sentenologist, not you. I'll keep my bargain with you, Jonuta. You may have the full thirty per cent of what you call my 'loot.'"

Jonuta leaned against the first mate's chair to his left. "Hear that, Kenny?" he said to the woman sitting there.

The chair rotated. In it sat a voluptuous woman with a large, more than attractive face and skin the hue of burnished bronze. She wore a truly lovely and obviously expensive sweater the color of champagne, with very full raglan sleeves decorated from collar to cuff by a braided plait of its own material. It bloused over her tight-hipped, tight-crotched but loose-legged pants, which were burnished burnt orange suede.

The sweater was cut lavishly, clear down to here, and the close-pressed cleavage made her look as if she was smuggling watermelons. She looked blandly at Marekallian Eks and up at her man, and nodded.

Jonuta looked back at Eks. "I'm the slaver here. I'm the one with the contacts and the knowledge to unload walking cargo right past watching security people. You only know how to fence artifacts."

"You're skipping one vital point, Jonuta."

"Which is?"

Marekallian Eks walked over to the con and looked squarely into Kislar Jonuta's dark, dark eyes.

"Phoenix is a living, thinking being that *I* found, freed, and took responsibility for. I'm not going to let you enslave him the same way TGO enslaves the worlds of the space-ways!"

Jonuta maintained a bland gaze and permitted himself a wry smile. *This poor flainer's obsession with fighting TGO is going to fob his thinking a little too much one of these days. Booda's eyeballs, he isn't even looking down into Kenowa's cleavage-canyon!*

"We've been fragged by a lot of action recently," the devilishly handsome master of *Coronet* said equably. "Some uninterrupted sleep will put us both in better mind to discuss this." He smiled and spread his hands placatingly.

To the great surprise of Verley of Sekhar, Marekallian Eks flipped his fingers in the spacefarer's equivalent of a shrug and said, "You're right. We're all on edge, Captain." He stretched his arms and stifled a yawn. "I think a few hours of horizontal meditation will work wonders."

*And that was about as transparent as your suggestion, Captain-san,* he mused without bitterness. *Now we'll see who corks whom, you smiling clone bastard!*

Eks spent the "night" portion of the spacer's sleep cycle wide awake.

Verley lay on the amorphous bed beside him, naked and relaxed, partly curled and wearing a disgustingly pleasant expression. She breathed regularly, asleep in a warm, post-lovemaking dreamworld. Well stroked and well fucked, Marekallian very well knew. The scent of their lovemaking titillated his nostrils still.

She twitched, sighed, turned to lie on her back. Naked and exposed with her emphatically straight pubic hair all tangled and still damp.

Without thinking about it Marekallian reached over to cup and squeeze a bare, softly relaxed breast—she made a happy sighing noise in her sleep—and gazed at the black grove between the tops of her thighs. It quite concealed her welcoming stash. Strange; most Galactics kept their bodies hairless from the eyelashes down, and nearly all from the neck down, at least. To do otherwise was to announce perversity—or the backward nature of one's culture.

He touched that soft, damp patch of fur and a little smile touched his face.

Marekallian Eks of Outreach positively reveled in backward cultures. His interest lay, however, along more serious lines than the avoidance of bald stash. He sought to bring new cultures into the interplanetary society of the universe, and he considered that every race's birthright.

Phoenix was the second representative of an *unknown* sentient species, and Eks was not about to let the Akil slip from his grasp.

(He had no notion that Jonuta had no intention of selling the Akil as a slave, and would not have cared to believe it had he known.)

A bumping sensation brought him to instant alertness and he withdrew his hands from the woman beside him. (Again she made a little sound, and again she turned away, onto her side, drawing her legs up.)

Eks smiled faintly. He knew the vibration a starship made when it hard-docked at a space station. Rolling gently off the bed, he eased his butt up and pulled on gray tights. Into them he stuffed a deep-rust hued shirt of grixsilk. He drew on his utilitarian jacket of Panishi khaki. It was well supplied with a score or so pockets that held items ranging from fifteen meters of coated monomolecular cable to a combination ministopper/jangler. His own full-sized stopper hung from the holster of the jacket's self-belt.

Sealing up the jacket's meld, he jumped lightly up and down to ensure that nothing rattled. *Firm*, he thought. *Not a sound*.

Eks slipped on leather boots and sealed their molecular bindings. Poised to leave, he glanced around the cabin for anything he might have forgotten.

Ah—he plucked his wristcomm up from the center table. He took a last look at the coiled, sleeping Verley 2197223SK of Sekhar.

She had followed him into the shrine tower of the Mother and her Lover—the gods of the Protected planet Arepien. And had helped him make off with its most exquisite artifacts. One was the Akil he called Phoenix. Verley had definitely been a life-saver.

*In the course of a long life,* he remembered, *a wise man must be willing to abandon his luggage many times*.

*Clear ether, my jacko!* He turned to open the hatch.

No sound disturbed the tunnel outside. Straining his hearing to its limits, Eks waited long moments before sealing the hatch as silently as he'd opened it. The soft leather boots moved as quietly as a whisper against the plasteel deck.

He heard them when he passed the second blowout pressure seal.

Kenowa had volunteered to take the Akil onstation. Jonuta had only to comm a holo of the beautiful alien to the first contact he'd picked. The price demanded and agreed to would buy a planet. Not a large planet, but hardly an asteroid, either.

Kenowa wanted one last moment with Phoenix...

The Akil sensed her need and readily made his affirmation apparent. Walking with him from the con to an empty cabin, she admired the growing size of the small alien's slim, long slicer. As with the rest of his beautiful, sensual body, his penis beckoned her with its promise of pleasure.

*"Makhseem,"* he whispered.

Kenowa smiled warmly. She'd heard him use the word often enough to presume that it was the Akil word for "fornicate." (That *makhseem* was infinitely more than fornication, she already knew—she had shared that marvelously intimate sexual bonding with the white-gold humanoid as often as she could during the flight to Jasbir. The Akil obliged, happy to spend its hours in a form of communication that required no words.)

The alien stroked Kenowa's firm backside, running its downy fingers into the valley between her cheeks as they walked with slow, languid steps.

*I'd buy Phoenix for me if I had the cred,* she thought. Feelings of tingly warmth pulsated through her. She walked faster. *That damn' cabin's too far. I might just take him right here in the tunnel and hope Sak and Shig are asleep. Vark, too, the Bleaker bum.* She knew Jonuta was wide awake, preparing the sale of Phoenix.

They turned at a tunnel junction and faced the Mindrunner.

Eks levelled his stopper at Kenowa and squeezed. He had it set on Two—Dance. Most men would have taken the opportunity to watch the magnificently endowed woman writhe and jerk under the effect of the sonic tingler. Her breasts trembled as if liquidly alive within her champagne-colored sweater and appeared to be trying very hard to burst and leap right out of its deep-cut U-front.

Instead of observing the arousing rictus, Eks swiftly pulled a short strap from one of his pockets and almost tried to grab her wrists with one hand while beaming her with the stopper in the other. He halted the action in time to avoid transmitting the effect of the beam to his own nervous system.

*Idiot,* he thought.

The Akil watched without alarm, his huge eyelids narrowed. Peering as a scientist would at a microbe.

Eks flicked off and holstered the stopper.

Kenowa stopped her Two-step Dance and sagged against a bulkhead. In the few seconds it took her jumbled nerves to begin approaching normalcy, Eks lashed her wrists together. He was careful to pass an end of the cord up between the linked wrists so as to tie them separately as well as together—and then he flipped the line over a standpipe, tugged it back, and knotted it three times.

Made helpless in less than a minute, she hung, arms over her head and the rather famous Kenowa breasts stretched tautly, sleekly lengthwise.

*The perfect damsel in distress,* Marekallian Eks thought, reaching up to pat her cheek.

"Sorry to leave you both unfulfilled and defenseless, supercake, but I have grander plans for Phoenix than his being a party favor."

"I don't blame you," she said in a tone both groggy and strained. And she added, "Jonuta will kill you for him, you know."

"Captain *Cautious?* I hardly think so, with me using Phoenix as a shield."

"That does show your concern for him, yes," she muttered.

But she was watching his back, and Phoenix's. Eks had departed with the Akil in tow without waiting to hear Kenowa's verdict on his ration of courage. She had a glimpse of Phoenix's slicer, shrinking from distraction and motion, and then of his very small very tight buttocks. Kenowa sighed.

She was aroused, in polite phrasing, and, in terminology less restrained, horny. Being in such a thoroughly kinky position made it worse. *And knowing that Marek is trying to escape with a great lover and a small fortune is even more frustrating!*

She did not intend to stay frustrated for long, and so did not dwell on it. She pressed her chin down between the shining tops of her forcibly elongated breasts.

"Jone," she said into her depthy cleavage. "Marek's got Phoenix. He must be heading for his lander. Verley wasn't with him."

Somewhere within her treasure chest, her wristcomm nestled warmly. Anticipating trouble, Jonuta had made the pleasant effort of assisting her in the secreting of her commlink. She cocked her head to listen.

*"Uh. I'm sending Vark and Shig to intercept."* Jonuta's voice barely reached up from the snug recess between her warheads. *"You check on Verley, Kenny. I do not want any surprises."*

"Uh, Jone . . ." Kenowa writhed, trying to unhook her wrists from the standpipe. "He's, uh, trussed me up."

*"I've got to stay oncon,"* her captain said. *"I'm sending Sak to free your trussworthy body, m'love. Enjoy it while you can."*

Kenowa smiled. The pain in her wrists diminished before the calm voice of her ever-competent man. She closed her eyes and tried to pretend that she was a prisoner here of that sublimely chivalrous but bondage-loving devil Captain Sword, who had long lived in her imagination.


The Akil stared at the hand that so firmly grasped his wrist. Marekallian tugged harder, urging him on toward the bay that held Eks's lander.

*"Sh'lashtiat kiz BavkaDil?"*

"Couldn't agree more," Eks said without listening. He

peered around a corner along a pale blue tunnel and ran at full gait to a sealed hatch. The alien called Phoenix must either run along behind or be dragged. He ran.

"This is it, fuzzface."

He punched the cycling switch on the hatch and waited all of two seconds before determining that it had been deactivated. Swiftly he unlatched the manual cycling bar and rotated it.

Footsteps sounded down the tunnel.

"Damn!"

The hatch eased slowly upward. Eks didn't waste time raising it more than a meter. Giving the Akil an ungentle shove down and under, Eks dived through the hatch after him and cycled it down from inside.

Spacefarer First Shiganu saw the hatch seal just as he rounded the corner. Vark stopped a pace behind him and cursed.

"Buggerhumpin' flainer's inside already! How the double vug're we supposed to get in there with the sisterslicin'–"

"Don't get fobbed," Shig said, raising his wrist. "They're inside the lander bay, Cap'm. Give the hatch some juice."

The only response was a whine as the hatch slid up. The Terasak and the Bleaker rushed into the empty airlock in time to see the pressure warning light flash orange.

"He's already evacuating the bay!"

*"He won't get far with the outer hatch sealed,"* came the voice of Captain Cautious, and it sounded oddly unselfassured.

*"Shree gast vo'tubriah!"* the Akil was meanwhile shouting, gesturing angrily.

Eks raised one hand placatingly while the other moved rapidly over the keys of his lander's inboard computer. He had kept the lander on a trickle charge so that it could be powered up in a few seconds.

"Relax and strap—oh shit." He reached over to nudge

the Akil into the other chair. "Get the drift?"

The Akil strapped in after watching Marekallian arrange his own safety gear. He settled back to stare at the Out-reacher with a distinctly human frown.

*"Give it up, Eks,"* a voice crackled over the intership comm. A voice deep and powerful. *"The hatch is zipped up tight and I'm overriding the pumps to repressurize the bay."*

"Just keep talking," Eks muttered under his adrenaline-accelerated breathing. He threw all power to one of the lander's more specialized and definitely customized acce-sories. The cabin lights dimmed.

A green beam of unbearable light blazed from the bow of the lander.

The burrowing laser burned a hole through *Coronet*'s outer hull in seconds.

*"You son of a sisterslicing—"*

"Uh-huh." Eks punched the laser off and the engines into throbbing life. Having torn a hole in Jonuta's beloved ship, *Golden Apple* shot past the hot glowing edges of the va-porized hatch and blasted away from *Coronet* and Jasbir-station.

Jonuta stood at the con, trembling in rage, ready to fire up DS. He hesitated. To harm the lander would be to harm the Akil. He couldn't do it. Telling himself it was because of the stell-value of the alien, he banged a fist down on the padded edge of the console and attacked the floating comm-mike with his voice.

"Sak! Vark! Get to the starboard lander and follow them. My bet is the bastard plans to drop down to the other side of the planet. Move move!"

# 3

Galactic population being what it is, it is safe to state that there are now *ten* suckers born *every second!*
—Ancient Outreacher Proverb

Eks's ingrav lander, *Golden Apple,* was neither golden nor apple-shaped. Its sleek, aerodynamic lines and coat of black, non-reflective pigment added to its speed and anonymity. Several modifications and additions of Eks's own design rendered the ship invisible to nearly all forms of detection. Onplanet or in space.

The lander's stubby wings bit air and caught on. He angled the dive steeply, using friction and retros to decelerate at a bone-grinding rate.

"That ought to lose those dragass flainers!" He ordered SIPACUM to pull out of the dive at one klom altitude and coordinate a landing at the city of Caraphyl. He turned to the Akil.

"Don't worry about a thing. I have friends in the city and we'll be off this dirtball in no time."

The Akil stared inquiringly. His fingers tapped with impatience against the chair-arm.

"And I'll fix you up so we can talk after we get a ship out of here." He glanced over at a bare spot on the alien's wrist. "Those scratch tests seem positive. You won't be allergic to a brainboost."

He cleared a landing pattern with Caraphyl StarHarbor

and entered a final approach pattern. The river-delta city spread out before them. Silver and gold spires of glittering crysplas shot up from banks (preserved in their natural, muddy condition). Elevated slideways connected the buildings and surrounding areas.

"And if we're lucky, we'll avoid the piss-petty burok that runs this planet."

Finding a freighter making the "short" hop from Jasbir to Suzi was simple. The run was a common one. Convincing the captain to make a stop at planet Sekhar proved to be more difficult. After the third try, Eks found hope with the fourth.

"Ya say yer want me to haul you and yer lander to Sekhar. That's it?"

Eks nodded.

"Isn't this a lot of cred to be paying for a little dogleg like that?"

Eks fingerflipped. "I despise haggling."

"Yer little jacko there coming too?"

Captain Saliandor da'Shiva looked down at the figure dressed in a garish tourmaline-green and interplanetary-orange keemo. It leaned against Eks, hanging its head low beneath a floppy crimson turban.

"Firm. Absolutely. Shipmate. My buddy!"

"Who's 'e?"

"Who, he?" Eks pulled the Akil closer so that the alien appeared to stumble. "He's, uh, drunk. Pos—can't even keep his head up. He'll spend the trip in my lander. Drying out. Don't worry about us. The boat's completely self-contained."

Captain Saliandor da'Shiva nodded his mahogny head and wordlessly accepted the stells Eks offered.

• • •

Eks found no trace of *Eris* around Sekhar. He suspected that his brother Denverdarian had been murdered there by agents (he assumed) of TransGalactic Order. He knew better than to nose around too boldly. One sweep of the planet with receptors scanning a special scrambled-and-digitally-encrypted wavelength confirmed what he'd already suspected. Geb Mardurki had taken his ship away from Sekhar, undoubtedly to Arepien.

Convincing Captain da'Shiva to detour to the far side of the Corsi Cluster required more than a few stells. Eks spent a good portion of a Sekhari week under a fake ID searching for a load of cargo that needed to be hauled to Terasaki, Luhra, or Rahman. He found a silicon component exporter with a shockingly expensive load of chips that needed to be offloaded at Luhra ASAP.

Captain da'Shiva happily agreed.

"And anytime yer want a position as ship's buyer," he told Eks, "I would be proud to have yer onboard!"

"Passage to Arepien will be sufficient."

"It's Protected..." The captain's voice betrayed hesitation.

Eks smiled his best golly-grabbles smile. "You'll hardly have to stop. Just give me enough time to redshift out of your lander bay and you can keep going. I'm good at short farewells." He added a wider smile.

Da'Shiva considered the probable risk, considered the possible profit, and smiled right back. "Enjoy the flight!"

Eks powered *Golden Apple* out of the airlock of *Yetzirah* and boosted toward one of the planets orbiting the binary stars Alkoman A and B. He turned to check on Phoenix's condition.

"You all right?"

The Akil wheezed and looked pathetically toward the Mindrunner.

"Sorry. I thought you'd take to the brainboosts more easily."

He flipped a few switches that rendered *Golden Apple* invisible to nearly every electromagnetic wavelength while at the same time beaming a message toward the planet on his select frequency.

"Feel sick," the Akil said in soft, weak Erts.

"It'll pass." Eks didn't bother scanning around the planet for *Eris*—he knew that Geb and Ashtaru had the spacer powered down and so completely shielded that it would be indistinguishable from an asteroid or any other cold, dark chunk of nothing-in-particular. Marekallian Eks preferred such anonymity.

"Geb, you flainer!" Eks commed. "I know you're out there. Better take the time to think up a good excuse for letting my brother get himself killed and redshifting Sekhar—"

*"I didn't think you'd get halfway across the Galaxy in a slipsucking lander, that's why!"* The voice was an angry tenor. *"You think we didn't suspect you were dead when we couldn't find any trace of you or your damned untraceable boat?"*

"Shut up and stand by for intercept. If you'd be so gracious as to give me a fix to home on."

*"Then what? Back down to Arepien?"*

"We head for the Council Redoubt."

*"Fine by me."*

A blip appeared on *Golden Apple*'s computer simulation of Arepien. He ordered SIPACUM to lock on to the commbeam and plot an interception course.

Onboard *Eris*, Eks ushered the Akil out of the lander and into the docking bay. Geb and Ashtaru—the only remaining members of the spacer's less-than-skeleton crew—stood at the hatch, waiting.

Ashtaru towered over Geb, though she stood only 155 sems,* with ebony black skin and hair dyed (currently) a screaming electric blue highlighted with turquoise and lavender streaks. She wore a lounger that matched the colors in top, belt, and bottom.

Geb barely topped her waist 100 sems off the deck. He glared up at Marekallian Eks and nocked his fists against his hips. He was that rarity along the spaceways—a genetic mistake, a *sport* left uncorrected *in utero* by impoverished parents. Geb Mardurki, midget, confronted his captain.

"Where in Theba's cold arms is the other lander?" Eks began.

"Lining a crater in its berth in Refuge. We had to sneak offplanet, thanks to Denvo's bungling. And if you'd stayed put onplanet according to plan, we'd have found you without a jinkle's effort. Stead, you somehow cross a few thousand parsecs without so much as—what the vug is *that?*"

The Akil looked down at the hurricane of verbiage, then at the striking Ashtaru (whose lounger did little to hide her taut, athletic body), then at his savior/kidnapper.

"I—" he struggled with the strange new language he had learned by virtue of Eks's encephaloboosts. "I am. . . . Klyjil bazRakava. Of Kuzih." He extended a downy golden hand to the Mindrunner. "I would like formally to thank you for rescuing me from my . . . cryosphere. I was en route from Kuzih to an outlying planet when forced to abandon ship. To close my eyes in deepspace and then open them in the arms of a beautiful alien woman amidst a flooding tomb was more than I could have . . . anticipated."

Eks shook Klyjil's warm hand and smiled. "Firm. Right. Thanks. Now we've got to be out of here and on the Tachyon Trail before we see a repeat of what happened the last time."

*And farewell, Verley. See you on those Scarlet Hills.*

---

*about 5 *feet* 1 *inch*, Old Style

• • •

"Damn it, Eks, stop staring at me like a fobbied gerbolansk!"

Eks stared at the Meccan for an awkward moment before
the image of Verley faded from his mind. Regaining his
bearings, he smiled thinly.

"Apologies, Veboranst. It's just that your speech was so
moving that—"

"I didn't say a word. The Eagler had the floor."

A murmur of amused annoyance flitted about the conference hall. *Damn,* Eks thought. *Let the mind wander a
second and the whole Rabble Alliance is down my throat.*
He lit a narcostick and rode out the interlude.

"Uh—I meant your speech to me. I wasn't aware that
your vocabulary included multisyllabic constructs." He
flicked ashes over the deck and addressed the Eagler. "I
think that after Veboranst's interruption, you deserve the
opportunity to restate your opinions. In brief."

The ruddy-skinned Eagler spoke for Tri-System Resistance. "We of the planets bound by the Tri-System Accord
are well acquainted with struggling to survive under the
burden of supporting not only TGO and TGW, but the Tri-
System Police as well. What Tri-System Resistance questions is the necessity of the Carnadyne Horde. Isn't the
Horde as much a drain on our resources as any of the tributes
we must pay to our oppressors?"

"Well put!" someone shouted.

"We're paying both ways!" another said.

A fist pounded against a table. All gazes turned toward
the sound.

Marekallian Eks held his fist in position on the table until
he was sure that he had everyone's attention. Slowly he
lifted it and pointed a finger at the Eagler.

"What the Council of Ninety-Three seems to forget is

that the Carnadyne Horde is a one-time expense, intended to be dismantled after use and put back into commercial service. Dreadnoughts and destriers are excellent for freight and mining operations. The Council was designed to be dismantled in the same manner—"

"And what's to prevent this council from *supplanting* TGW, TGO, and all the others?" a Thebanian woman in a maroon jellabah asked in a voice like wind through a crystal forest.

*This is as much a pain as organizing Protected natives,* Eks thought, and said equably, "Control here is not centralized as it is in every known form of governmental tyranny. We have no Boss—*by design.* Any one of you who wishes to take on the task of organizing your own movement is free to do so. Any who join you will do so because they judge your methods to be better than anyone else's." He paused, looking around the room.

"Hearing no offer to take up this venture, I'd like to point out the one problem with the Carnadyne Horde. The Horde is as necessary to us as a stick is necessary to fend off an attacking chulwar. And when we have convinced enough planets to divert their wealth away from TGO, that gang of thieves will behave like the beast of prey it is.

"TGO, however, is not yet starving. The Carnadyne Horde is premature." Eks inclined his head toward an astonishingly tall man sitting three seats to his left. "With all due respect to Master Strategist Surdiakah, it is impossible to *start* a revolution. One is certain to lose. Only when we have enough planets on our side will there be a revolution. And the violence will come from TGW. Governments—through their military and police—will invariably resort to violence as their last ditch effort to retain their power. Until then, they have the legitimized 'consent' of their citizens and—"

"Is there a point to this histrionics lesson, Marek?" The Master Strategist glowered at Eks.

They looked levelly eye-to-eye with one another even though one stood and the other sat.

"Time, Surdiakah. In time I can have enough Protected planets totally on our si–"

Surdiakah laughed in deep mockery.

"Again you plague this council with your pitiful scheming. We all know that your Mindrunning takes second place to your grave-robbing. We gratefully accept the funds thus generated, but the idea that pre-space *barbarians* can contribute anything to a revolution against a technologically superior and devious enemy is less than ridic–"

*Fool!* Eks took a deep breath and slowly straightened to lift his fists from the table.

"*Myrzha* Surdiakah," he said, "I have always considered the Council of Ninety-Three to be composed of persons who place individual freedom above all other considerations. What could be more oppressive than to prevent the movement of knowledge between sovereign minds?"

"The contribution of primitives to our resistance would be minuscu–"

"They wouldn't be primitives by the time I got through with them!" Marekallian Eks turned to address the the entire chamber. "Friends and comrades," he began.

"Oh, Booda," Surdiakah moaned.

"This revolt against tyranny must not be tainted by elitist preconceptions about the worth of *any* sentient being. For me, the largest fleet in the Galaxy would be worthless if no one knew what it was fighting *for*. The collapse of the Empire proved *that!* Guerilla tactics and education are what we require. Combined with the systematic evasion of TGW, TAI, and TSP enforcement and extortion, we can prove to the doubtful that they can survive *and thrive* without the 'protection' of this proto-empire."

"Does your wearisome aria have a conclusion?" The Master Strategist stared at Eks with a jaundiced gaze.

*Pos. First, however, you get the cadenza.* "Only this. If the yoke of TGO is ever to be thrown off our necks, we need popular support. That requires publicity, not secrecy."

A murmur circulated through the crowd.

Eks held a finger up. "Every time a smuggler evades a policer or a bureaucrat is roughed up by an angry citizen, the fact should be played up. Some news services admire that roguish aspect of spacefarers."

"This is a revolution," a squat Andran shouted, "not a holomeller!"

"Revolution," Eks countered, "is show business. No one will notice it otherwise! If the masses don't see what we're doing to help them, they won't care a flaining jinkle about joining us!"

The Outie turned and stormed out of the chamber.

Surdiakah—Master Strategist—rose up to his full height of over two meters and raised a hand for silence. "If," he said, "there are no other interruptions, I trust we can get back to matters of a more—*realistic* nature..."


*Damned short-sighted, intellectually incestuous militarist* bastards!

Eks trod past the pressure seals in the space station's spoke and strode into the umbilical connected to *Eris*. He thumbed the hatch.

"Ash!" he shouted, knowing that the inship comm to the airlock switched on whenever the hatch cycled. His hair whipped about as he looked up at the speaker grill. "Ash?"

*"Not oncon, Marek."* Geb sounded annoyed.

Eks opened the inner hatch and continued to speak.

"Get the ship ready to redshift. Inslot a course to Lanatia." He took a left turn down a walnut-and-prass lined tunnel and headed toward the con-cabin.

*"Why Lanatia? I thought the Council would be meeting for the rest of the week."*

Eks reached the con and addressed Geb face to face. "We're going to contact an investigative reporter for *Galactic News* and take it with us on a mindrunning expedition."

"What?" Geb stared up at his captain in shock.

"Kabeshunt. It's near Murph. Protected. The natives are very close to achieving spaceflight. One little push from us and they'll be all over the spaceways. That should make a great story."

Geb turned back into the mate's chair and touched his small hand against the stopper holstered on his thigh. He frowned. "I don't think I understand. We've always kept a zero-low profile."

"Ask me later. Got the course inslotted?"

"Firm."

"Where's Klyjil?"

"He's, uh, occupied with Ash."

Eks nodded without smiling. Switching on the inship comm, he said, "Attention all crew. Prepare for departure in ten mins and acceleration out to safe point for subspace entry in one half-hour. Repeat—SPOSE in thirty mins. Destination Lanatia."

He looked at Geb. "That ought to give them time to . . . disengage."

# 4

You can't go home again. And if you do, don't expect to
find any fatted calves.

—Marekallian Eks

Space is long, and wide, and deep. And space is achingly
*dark*. The great darkness threatens to overwhelm what little
light there is in the universe and in the expectations of
humans. Yet, the dark is nothing. It is the light that is
everything. Many have looked into the light-spattered darkness of space and seen reflected there the human soul.

It was easier, in toward the center of the Galaxy. There
humans had ever seen a light, a Light; a great murky glow
that reminded ancients of spilled and spattered milk, so that
they called it the Milky Way . . . Galaxy, in their language.
There lies the core of the enormous spiral of stars and their
attendant planets; there the stars are thick as gravel on a
rural road at election time. Far and far from that glowing
Galactic center lay the star called Sol, with its planets. The
race of sentient beings that grew and grew on Sol's third
planet, Homeworld now, were drawn to the Light. They
left their world, they left the confines of their rural sun and
headed in, in toward the Galactic core and its gray hazy
light.

The light was of stars uncounted, stars of a dozen hues
and more sizes.

Here humankind had found that light and warmth it sought, so that the blackness was not, but was no less than grayness, at the least. Humans settled the star-worlds that seemed so much closer to the center of Creation. (So they told themselves, ignoring the fact that theirs was one of many, many galaxies, all vastly far apart and all star-crammed, all with centers. . . .)

This is ours, humankind said, and renamed itself. It became the Galactic race. It inhabited the brightness of planets and the great sun-strewn twilight between the worlds it settled.

One of those suns was Hubble and another was Durga, and they were companions. One of their planets was settled, and Galactics named it Terasaki.

Through the eternal twilight of space shot a graceful, powerful ship called *Sunmother*—a name not rooted in the history and legends and superstitions of the Galactic race. *Sunmother* raced toward the planet Terasaki.

On that star-world, in an apt in the city of Yamato, a woman alone traveled through her own universe of darkness and light.

*The most evil of villains,* she thought, *believe in good, in the Good. No one can consider herself alone and remain sane; no one can consider herself evil and survive long, let alone function.*

She shifted her position from Siddhasana to Veerasana. From the adept's pose to that of the warrior. A joint or three of her spine popped.

The woman called Kalahari Cuw paid that no heed.

*I've done a lot of things that certainly were wrong.* (She breathed with almost catatonic slowness.) *Hell. I very well knew they were wrong when I did them, too. I reveled in that! I thought they were justified—or pretended to. And I've done right things. Good things. (Some.) Does that make me evil or good? Or both? Or neither?*

*It makes me good-evil and evil-good. Gray.*

*It makes me human.*

The very lean woman unwrapped her body and raised up on her forearms to bring her legs over her head and into the Vrischikasan—the scorpion pose. Toes attempted to touch head and nearly succeeded.

*I've done worse than some and better than most. If any of my acts required punishment in the eyes of gods or Galactics, I surely received enough on Jorinne and Knor.\**

*And got off rich!*

A chime sounded. Kalahari Cuw unwound her body and stared at the door. Peatmoss Nebula-gray hair framed her eyes, subcutaned a deeper shade of gray. She wore no clothes while meditating and didn't bother to reach for any.

"Who!" she demanded of the door. A Looker switched on, giving her a TP view of the hallway outside the apt.

Four figures snugly clad in red stood on the other side of the door.

"Oh shit." Kalahari stood slowly, her gaze never drifting from the Looker.

She was a lean woman. Small breasts and narrow hips accentuated the sleek muscles of her legs and arms. She walked to the door, though she could have addressed them as easily from the exercise mat.

She pressed her body against the door, leaning an ear against its cool surface.

"What?" she asked quietly.

"Kalahari?" a man's voice said. "It's the Satana Coalition."

"I know." The Looker carried her voice to a speaker in the hallway. Even so, it sounded restrained.

"We need–" Trafalgar Cuw paused and gazed up at the

---

*Spaceways #8, #9 and #4: *Under Twin Suns, In Quest of Qalara,* and *Satana Enslaved*

Looker TP. "I mean—we *want* you. Come and help us look for Janja."

The door opened. Kalahari Cuw—the former pirate Hellfire—faced her friends, unashamed (or unaware) that she was naked.

"Sis!" Trafalgar Cuw flashed her the familiar boyish smile.

The Jarps Sweetface and Cinnabar stood behind him. One wore a translahelm, the other didn't. Behind them stood a subdued woman with skin the color of obsidian. Quindarissa looked at her former captain and smiled warmly, quietly. All of them wore red jumpsuits sashed in black at the waist. All were form-fitting.

"You don't need my help. As for what you want..." Kalahari spoke with detached calm. "I'm afraid I won't be much help or even very good company. I'm—learning— these days. It takes up all my time. There's so much that I don't know..."

"Hellf—" Quindy reached out an arm like soft onyx toward her friend and lover. "We haven't found her yet. We had leads. Traf is great at finding things out. When we left you, we went to Nevermind, Samanna, Lanatia."

Every time, the story had been the same. The descriptions came back more or less the same: "Small woman? Hair like a summer's cloud? Saw her with three men. Stayed a few days."

"Eyes like frozen diamond? She look odd, yah. Miss her by two weeks."

"That big spender? Scandalously pink skin! Came off *Hindilark,* I'm told. Spent a fortune, then just as quickly redshifted. I *knew* she was trouble—not nobility at all!"

The last had confused the four who quested for Janja. Trafalgar Cuw had followed a hunch or "hunch" and traced the Aglayan to Samanna. Yet at a stopover on Lanatia, he had encountered this perfect description of her.

"We don't know where she went from there," Quindy

told her former captain. "Even Traf couldn't find out who owned *Hindilark,* or how she got onboard."

Trafalgar Cuw smilingly spread his hands and shrugged in uncharacteristic admission of uncharacteristic helplessness—about anything.

"It's just that—" Cinnabar's words caught in its throat and implanted translator. If a Jarp could stammer, the whistling sound Cinnabar made would qualify. "We just want you *back.* We miss you."

The others nodded in an embarrassed silence. They anxiously watched the gray and tan woman in the doorway.

"I was never a good captain," Kalahari said slowly. "You all know that. I've been a detriment from the start and I marvel at how I've lasted this long. I have a lot to learn before I'm worth anything to anybody. Especially to me."

Trafalgar laid a hand lightly on her shoulder. She didn't shrug it off as she might have in the past. "Take all the time you want to learn. Take everything you need. Just do it on *Sunmother.* With us."

Kalahari Cuw regarded her comrades for a moment, then gestured them inside. "I'll probably stay in my cabin."

"You won't have any duties," Quindy urged. "No one will interfere."

The thin woman who had been Captain Hellfire was not immune. She licked her lips. Gray eyes shifted to look from Quindy to Trafalgar to the Jarps. She saw only friends, and her eyes kindled.

"Let me get dressed."

"Uh—we brought you something . . ."

The box Cinnabar handed her contained a stretch-fab jumpsuit, red, and a long black sash. Kalahari Cuw managed not to cry.

Within less than a half-hour, all four crimson-clad members of the Satana Coalition—with the identically jumpsuited Sweetface—were on their way to the spaceport.

• • •

The days passed quietly. *Sunmother,* piloted by the master ship-handler Quindy, plunged in and out of "subspace" to wend its way through the gravitic landscape of the Galaxy. Stars fled by in every color and variation from radio to gamma. At the behest of the ever-enigmatic Trafalgar Cuw of Outreach, they were headed for Mirjam out past Barbro.

A few days and hundreds of light years from the planet, Quindy asked the Satana Coalition to meet in the con-cabin.

They found her wearing a royal blue bandeau and matching pants, very soft and loose.

"This is something I can't choose on my own," she told them. She looked at each member of the crew by turn. "Between us and our destination lies the Carnadyne Void. We can either shift to standard drive and take our sweet time pushing through that cosmic rock-and-dust quarry or we can take my shortcut."

"Roche's Alley?" Sweetface whistled a meaningless, untranslatable phrase and shifted from one foot to the other.

It referred to the gap between the two collapstars named Skylla and Karybdis by some sanguine astrocartographer. Maneuvering along the constantly shifting geodesic between the "black holes" with less than half a light year on either side was Quindy's idea of fun. Most spacefarers daring (or plain stupid) enough to attempt threading that needle were now loose atoms and crackling ions, drawn toward one dead star or the other and torn apart by tidal forces.

Quindarissa flipped five to Sweetface.

"I've done it five times," she said in a flat statement of fact. "The nice thing about it is that Skylla and Karybdis keep Roche's Alley swept clear of debris. Just a pair of big ole magnets, sucking everything up. Shoot through there now and we cut three days off our trip."

The captain of *Sunmother* scratched absently at her right breast in a massage of the aureole beneath her bandeau. The slim quartz ring piercing that shiny halo of flesh (compliments of her Knorese slavemaster after their escape from planet Macho and crashdown on Knor) kept the nipple larger than its mate. It didn't hurt, and Trafalgar liked it. But sometimes the flesh surrounding the damned thing itched.

Trafalgar watched her and smiled. He liked that so-slim circle of quartz, and he loved those breasts. He'd have his hands on them again shortly, when he and the jonquil-haired, dyed-by-her-own-hand black woman retired to a shared bed. They gave each other what each wanted. What Quindy wanted—and needed—as part of her sexuality was mastery, roughness. She had gotten it from Hellfire, and she got it from Trafalgar Cuw—with less harshness. He had *known* it, that first time.* Their sexual preferences were nicely complementary.

"If we can catch up to Janja," Cinnabar was saying without hesitation, "it's worth the risk, isn't it?"

Quindy glanced around for dissenters, found none, and smiled. She turned to the con.

Deft black fingers danced over the keys, alerting SI-PACUM to their proposed course change. Telits flashed in eye-eez turquoise to acknowledge receipt of the orders. Other console lights came alive, in five colors, as if bragging of the actuation of this and that system and the performance of this function and that.

"I think we done decided," Trafalgar Cuw said, with a smile in his voice. "You don't have a cassette for this run, I hope."

Quindy smiled, too. "No cassettes for this trip. The way these two collapstars orbit their common point makes a

_____

SPACEWAYS #3: *Escape from Macho*

damnably tricky curve of the geodesic necessary to pass between them. I like to hit the interface at about point nine-oh-five $\overline{c}$. That gives me enough kick on the far side—"

She glanced around and her sensuous lips spread in a grin. Fingers flipped in the "who cares?" gesture. "Well, you know. We'll get there." And she swung back to her instruments and calculations.

A short time later they were in trouble. Bad trouble.


No spacer was perfect. Ask any spacefarer. And a new spacecraft had a breaking-in period that was more often than not a breaking-down period. Usually this resulted in noting more than a few muttered curses and a delay in flight time.

Not this time.

Trafalgar Cuw muttered a curse and struggled to contain his apprehension. He pulled the crysplas chipboard from the guts of the con. Quindy worked furiously at the backup console.

"Which way are we drifting?" he asked.

"Toward Skylla. You know—'left.' Point-oh-three degrees per minute by the second derivative."

"Wonderful," the man from Outreach said. The collapsed star on the port side of *Sunmother* was drawing them toward its ravenous event horizon at an increasing angle every instant. He threw the chipboard aside.

"This one's fried, Quin. And it caused a power spike to hit the quanta oscillation damper. The TDP couldn't handle the glitch and shut down the whole dam' drive."

"Uh-huh. I read only attitude rockets as functional. And there's sure no SPOSE near *these* mass-suckers."

"We could go Forty Percent City."

Quindy tried to grin and looked as if it hurt. "The odds aren't that bad yet. Check the MVRD unit."

He poked a circuit analyzer at the board requested. "Green. No fobs."

The spacer lurched. Trafalgar looked up at Quindy. "Tidal effects already?"

"Can't be. I think the drive's starting to spark."

"Theba's thighs—not until I get the replacement board in!" He scrambled for the new chipboard.

"Well, I don't have any control over–"

She was interrupted by another tremble of the ship. Red telits flashed their warnings. "What's wrong?" she asked the con.

The calm voice of the computer and guidance system installed by ship's owner Janjaglaya Wye, who had experienced a vocally interactive computer on Jorinne and just had to have one, explained:

"The double-P engines are experiencing intermittent venting. The seals are in danger of damage unless the venting can be arrested."

"Got to reprogram that damned thing not to say 'arrested,'" Trafalgar Cuw muttered.

Quindy brushed back a strand of canary-yellow hair. "Can your cybers stop the venting?"

"Neg."

She toed the Outie gently with her boot. "It's down to the engine room for us. We've got to shut the vents manually. And fast."

He nodded and stood, brushing dust off his gold-and-ruby keemo. He picked up his broad-brimmed Wayne and slapped at its edges before clapping it on his head.

"Why don't we do just that, Captain Quindy ma'am. Without a quanta oscillation damper or a TDP, it's going to take a few hours to rig up something to get us going again."

She made an unpleasant face. "By then we'll be stardust."

He hummed a sub-ancient melody and smiled. "Maybe ole Cag has some sort of suggestion."

"You might be able to request your necessary items,"

the CAGSVIC IV unit stated in its sickeningly courteous voice, "from the spacer approaching off the stern at one-eight-one."

*"What?!"* Both of them looked at the CAGSVIC's TP "eye" out of reflex action.

"It masses out as an ultralight freighter. Should I initiate contact?"

"Pos!"

"Firm! Send a *C!* message and make it a double-*C!* for more than urgent! Traf—get down to the drive chamber!" She bent over the con and switched on the aft receptors and the inship comm. "Cinnabar: relieve me at the con. We've got company." Watching the computer simulation of the other spacer, she muttered, "All right, little jacko, where are *you* going in such a hurry?"

Trafalgar Cuw paused in his departure to look back at her and smile. Not only at the way her upturned stern assembly tightened those loose royal blue pants.

*Fine,* he thought with pleasure. *She's starting to behave like the captain she's supposed to be. A captain that can and will get us out of this.* He raised his gaze to the computer simulation of Skylla and their diminishing distance from that ever-ravenous black mouth.

*That is, if we live long enough.*

# 5

Man can survive in an inclement universe only through the
use of his mind. His thumbs, his nails, his muscles and his
mysticism will not be enough to keep him alive without it.
                                    —Karl Hess, *The Death of Politics*


A HRal was a rare sight. Unless one of them wore a m/ss
or bundled up in a sektent, a felinoprimate was hard to miss.

The *two* HRal onboard *Taras Bulba,* then, were an Event.
And both HReenee and HRadem revelled in the attention.

HReenee and her step-sib HRadem had shipped out with
the rowdy crew of asteroid miners when word of the death
of Kislar Jonuta reached her on Qalara.* She knew that
Kenowa would never permit her back onboard *Coronet,* so
the two contracted out on the first available spacer. She had
been badly shaken. Jonuta was a man HReenee both re-
spected and liked, more than a little.

"Yer know," one of the less grimy miners said to her,
smiling, "you look real good in Galactic clothes. I kin count
eight of ya' bitty nipples on ya' eight bitty warheads when
yer stretch like that."

HReenee stiffened, then pulled back in from her pantherish elongation. Her cerulean reelsilk shirt, cut in an ancient pirate style, slid in ripples over her long chest. Each
nipple showed as a tiny nub atop a small mound. She ad-

---

*Spaceways #9: *In Quest of Qalara*

justed the folds of her deep purple *jurl*—loose HRal pants—
and resumed her meal. The miner sat next to her in the mess
hall of *Taras Bulba*.

HRadem was at her left, eyeing a busty, butsy woman
in a bright yellow SpraYon body-stocking. He smiled. HRadem had not spent a night alone in the ship's month he had
been on the spacer. Neither had HReenee. The women her
brother trysted with relished his forceful, violent lovemaking. They went positively ecstat over his feverish HRal body
temperature.*

HReenee pretended to ignore the miner on her right. She
didn't object to his overtures any more than she would object
to an animal's rubbing against her leg. Just small-man crude-
ness, but . . . interspecies sex intrigued her, as it intrigued
most spacefarers. And Jonuta was gone, gone. Unlike the
majority of Galactics, she didn't require sentience of her
partner. This miner adequately fitted that description, and
didn't *mean* to insult.

He was merely stupid, crude and callous. Merely.

HReenee demurred with a sexy flip of her fingers. The
gesture—when performed by a HRal—caused her single,
retractile claw to extrude from her middle finger.

The miner quietly turned back to his meal. He knew as
well as anyone else on *Taras Bulba* that HReenee had made
her choice of cabinmates. And that choice would be re-
spected. She slept in the bed of Captain Darkblood.

She finished eating and leaned back in her chair. Her
eyes—evolved for a hunting race—gazed to survey the
crowd.

*So intent on their small concerns.*

She slid her tray into the disposall and purred something
in the language of HRal to her step-sib, nodding in the
direction of the spacefarer he'd been eyeing.

---

*About 104 degrees *Fahrenheit*, Old Style.

HRadem smiled slyly and stood to follow the woman in yellow. His partner for the night was virtually assured.

HReenee's partner was assured absolutely. She headed for the exit, her fluid motions drawing many a miner's gaze. Those who watched knew her destination. Some resented the captain for its good fortune. Others resented HReenee for hers. And some tried lasciviously to imagine their captain with the HRal.

HReenee thumbed the hatch to the captain's cabin. Only her right thumbprint—or any of Captain Darkblood's four— could actuate the lock. The plasteel barrier slid aside silently.

Her sensitive nostrils detected the almost subliminal odor of pheromones and other body scents. A tingle of anticipation prickled at her flesh, raising her fur. She thrilled at the aroma of her lover. It was so... *different*. Different from the scent of HRal or Galactic.

Captain Darkblood emitted the pheromones of both a male and a female.

*"Whhherrrl?"* HReenee thumbed the hatch shut and glided across the cabin to the study.

Captain Darkblood sat at the room's terminal, staring at a SIPACUM computer simulation of the asteroid that *Taras Bulba* was towing. Fingers tapped against the chair arm, first a thumb, followed by each of four fingers in turn, followed by the opposing thumb. Its orange skin looked less orange and more reddish in the screen's light.

Darkblood took a deep breath to savor the delicious perfume of the HRal's arrival before turning around to face her. The Jarp smiled.

"T'lee?" it whistled in a deep, thrumming tone, pleasant but strong.

HReenee made a gesture with her hands. They seemed to entwine and then rise and spread out like a flower in bloom.

Captain Darkblood understood the gesture. On its native Jarpi, gestures were seldom translatable as words and more often were gifts. Darkblood accepted the gift with a gesture of its own and rose to take her in its arms.

Captain Darkblood was an enigma even in the variegated, turbulent Galaxy where nothing shocked or surprised. Though well known to anyone around the spaceports and mining worlds frequented by *Taras Bulba,* Darkblood lived a life of adventure that few believed and even fewer could dream of experiencing.

Born on Jarpi, sold into slavery at an early age, Darkblood might have lived out its life as yet another of millions of Jarps. A slave of Galactic masters.

The young Jarp refused to accept submission.

It was prized as an amusement and a sexual toy. Like all Jarps, it was a true hermaphrodite, possessing both a testicle and an ovary, a penis and vagina. Darkblood—who in those days had been called Knobbles because of its larger than normal breasts (for a Jarp)—had been abused, humiliated, raped, and occasionally tortured. Its master—a Thebanian politician—had raped it both hetero- and homosexually.

Knobbles didn't object to the sex as much as it objected to the *trespass*. That it was forced to engage in such acts with a partner it despised, under threat of death, was the source of its hatred.

One night the Jarp's master died in an unpleasant manner that caused his political cronies to whisper the letters TGO.

His less-than-adored son inherited most of the politician's wealth, including the Jarp. One day, the orange-skinned slave presented its new owner with an alarming sum of money. It demanded to buy its freedom. (The money was stolen by deft, slender Jarp fingers. Its master knew this, but there was enough that he didn't mind.) He set Knobbles free.

The damned brooding orange thing made him *nervous*. Knobbles swore never again to be a slave to anyone.

The first Galactic that tried to enslave it again met with a surprisingly gruesome death. The Reshi (in a Thebanisport bar) had not expected a "mere" Jarp to own a knife truncheon or know how to swing it.

The Jarp owned one and had learned its use well. The seven razor-thin titanium blades on the business end of the meter-long truncheon bit and slashed and ripped.

Knobbles had earned a new name. The witnesses to the fight confirmed to the policers that the Jarp had acted in self-defense. They had been more impressed with its fighting skill than with any consideration of its civil or individual rights.

They saw the cold, vicious look in the alien's eyes when it *placidated* the Reshi. Its normally sweet brown eyes— wide and round—had narrowed to dark, blood-lustful slivers.

Knobbles walked out of the bar as Darkblood, still free. Vehemently free! The next mining spacer to leave Thebanis had onboard it a strong, no-nonsense Jarp who worked hard for its pay.

Over the years, Darkblood had earned its wealth in ways honest and hard (and sometimes not so honest, yet still hard).

HReenee appreciated her captain's strength of character and powerful sense of purpose. It felt at no disadvantage to be a Jarp among Galactics. It felt quite the opposite, articulating what most Jarps seldom said aloud.

"I can be a man or a woman to anyone of any sex," it had told HReenee after an evening in which it had been both to her. "If these Galactics could experience sexuality from both sides—complete with hormonal influences—they would finally see that the way they treat each other is so thoughtlessly cruel and petty."

HReenee agreed. She had learned more about Galactics from this Jarp than from all her time with Pentamahomet Ramzi and Kislar Jonuta. And understanding Galactics was vital to Mranophel HReenee sa'fiel, who posed as a researcher of linguistics.

Now HRal and Jarp embraced. HReenee ran her sensuous hands over Captain Darkblood's powerful muscles—stronger than any Jarp's and many a human's. Her captain wore its usual outfit of emerald-sheen skinTites from waist to moroccan equhyde boots that topped just below the knees. The matching belt wrapped around its lean waist supported a stopper holster and loop for the knife truncheon it still owned and carried. Its tight rust-hued top (long-sleeved) clung to its sleekly muscled arms and firm round breasts.

Darkblood took great pride in its body, choosing also to accentuate the bulge of its male organ by means of the skinTites. The Jarp gave the first impression of being an alluringly athletic woman. It wore its deep ruby hair long and in a single, barbaric braid down its back. The translahelm it wore to converse in Erts fitted snugly over the hairstyle. (Though it could well afford the expensive operation, the captain of *Taras Bulba* trusted no one to implant a translator surgically.)

Orange fingers stroked at HReenee's four pair of small, downy breasts. Twin thumbs pinched each nipple in succession. They firmed up beneath the loose reelsilk shirt.

She looked into the eyes of her lover. Eyes gold as a yellow sun gazed at cool brown eyes as round as saucers. Slowly, with an esthete's grace, she slid out of her shirt and *jurl*. She moved her downy body against her captain's with a sensuous writhing of her breasts against its. A slender, long-nailed hand snaked down to grasp the firm slicer pressed between them.

Suddenly she released her grip and pulled away. A HRal woman had to be *taken*.

Darkblood knew this. It enjoyed the conquest. Most Galactic women, it found, were too amenable—too softly acquiescent. HRal women demanded that a lover prove itself.

The Jarp had spent its life proving itself.

It pounced to seize her—and grabbed air. She stood a couple of meters away, smiling. Ears covered with soft fur twitched with teasing playfulness. Her eyes were bright, anticipating . . .

Her pursuer faked a dive to the left and shot an arm out to encircle her wrist. One savage tug brought her to the bed.

Her supple, felinoid body was mostly legs and she used them. One kick and she snared her lover's neck. Thighs squeezed against throat, crushing.

With a mighty arch of its back, the Jarp flung both of them forward and onto the bed. They bounced once and a slim, pointed tongue worked its way into the valley at the apex of her legs.

Her hands grasped at the braid snaking over her leg and tugged.

Her "assailant" pulled back in surprise. It stood, six-fingered hands stripping off clothing with quick motions.

"This time you'll surrender or be—oof!"

She used her captain's abdomen for a convenient point from which to kick off, grinning. Yet before she could sail clear, a hand darted to her ankle, clamped, and swung.

HReenee landed on the bed. Darkblood landed atop her.

She made a throaty purring sound, reaching down to stroke the rock-hard, insistent organ that demanded entry. Slender fingers stroked the penis—large for a Jarp's—and lightly scratched at its testicle. Edging deeper, they explored the cool (to a HRal) interior of her lover's other sex.

Feeling the feverishly hot touch of HRal fingers inside its tight stash, the Jarp whistled a low, lustful note. In one swift motion, it withdrew her hand, pinioned them both to the bed, and slid a knee between her legs.

It pounced. Its questing slicer found the way to her waiting vulva, and in.

She struggled. Her lover, though, possessed the strength
of one accustomed to hand combat—as she knew.

It enjoyed the way she fought. Her exertion filled the air
of the cabin with a love-scent that intoxicated the Jarp's
sensitive nostrils unto drunkenness.

She squirmed beneath her conqueror, now taken as she
needed to be and fully in its thrall. Nipples swelled, engorged and purplescent with blood. Her straw-gold fur
stroked against the full length of her captain's body. Her
tongue curled out from between thin lips to tease at her
lover's breasts. She savored the taste of salt and the smooth
texture of the bright orange lobes.

While her lover drove into her with ever-deeper thrusts,
she insinuated her hand back between its tensing legs. She
slipped one finger into its female half and a thumb into its
rectum.

It gasped in pleasant surprise at the massaging motions
her fingers made. The sensation only made more urgent its
drive into her truly hot loins.

With every stroke of the alien above her, the HRal set
up her own counter-rhythm of sinuous motion. Her short,
downy fur rubbed against her lover's flesh and against the
coral Panishi sheets.

Somewhere deep within her, a purr began. In all the
millions of years of evolution on HRalix, her race had not
lost that soothing, intimate trait of its ancestors.

Her body's fever-heat (and deft fingers) drove the Jarp
onward to an explosive, shuddering flash. The sudden flood
of cool, cool seed produced a shiver that grew into a moan-
ing, shaking climax.

Somewhere far away, SIPACUM *ping*ged gently. HReenee barely heard it. Captain Darkblood heeded it only to

note that it indicated the approach of *Taras Bulba* to the planet called Front.

*Ahh*, thought the richest Jarp in the Galaxy (except possibly for Cinnabar of the Satana Coalition) *commerce and carnality. The two greatest achievements of sentient life!*

Darkblood nestled its two large warheads against four of HReenee's and breathed deeply of their lovemaking. *Who needs Galactics?*

# 6

... a secret government is little less than a government of
assassins. Under it, a man knows not who his tyrants are,
until they have struck, and perhaps not then.

—Lysander Spooner
*No Treason*

The woman in black sat in the crowded, smoky bar hating
the man who'd assigned her to it. She tried to look sexy
amid the squalid surroundings. Graha, the capital of Front,
had a population of less than eleven thousand. Tonight most
of them seemed to have decided to crowd into Daraki's
Demonhole Bar.

Daraki sat in an alcove at the back, watching the evening's action with patriarchal joy. The stells were flowing
freely tonight. The night the mining ships arrived.

Daraki was a stout man. Oh, he used the decaloric en-
zyme, he merely underused it a bit. Daraki allowed himself
a body thick enough to withstand the punches of nearly any
drunken customer, yet not so thick that women would find
him unattractive.

Front being the planet it was, inhabitants considered bar-
owners to be missionaries and saints of Theba, Booda, and
Musla all in one.

Daraki gazed at the crowd of spacefarers and locals
through a pair of darkeyes that were actually TP receptors.

56

TP cameras, cleverly disguised in the ceiling, watched the entire barroom with greater ability than even the sharp-sighted Fronter could accomplish. Their special optics cut through smoke and ambient light to give Daraki a complete overview of his operation. The smoke was easily dispelled. Daraki had *chosen* that the Demonhole Bar be smoky . . . to everyone but him. He had even wired the brothel upstairs.

Purely for security, of course.

He turned his TP attention to table number 17. There sat a vision unlike any he'd ever seen on Front or in any of the holoporn discs he'd perused.

She was unique: *une type*. Thus, her very appearance was shocking, in an altogether positive way. The sort of woman who collected stares—and ignored them.

In a Galaxy where natural skin hue varied from light brown or yellow to very nearly-and-sometimes-definitely black, in a time when natural eye color passed through shades of brown to black, among a race called Galactics to whom any hair color lighter than hazel or copper was nearly unknown, this woman stunned all about her with hair and skin and eyes so unlike theirs.

She sat alone at a table for two, Daraki noted to his mild annoyance (seats were at a premium tonight). Men—more densely-packed than elsewhere in the bar—crowded around her to stare while trying not to appear to do.

Her hair was the color of a distant GO star, almost an achromatic white. Her eyes possessed the gray color of summer clouds troubled by a hidden, building storm. And her skin—her skin.

Daraki thought that her skin exceeded the promise of the Garden of Musla in its beauty. He quickly prayed an apology for such a thought and zoomed in the TP image for a closer view.

Skin a lightly-tanned pink. Impossible! Yet the color could not have been so convincingly subcutaneous as to fool the bar-owner's discerning sight. Her flesh was that color once outrageously referred to as "flesh-colored" by a minority of humans on a planet called Urth—Homeworld to the race called Galactics. (A race no longer "flesh-colored" by the appalling standards of that extinct sub-race!)

This woman—who might also once have been called "white"—sat nursing a drink, oblivious to the attention paid her. That she concentrated on her plass of good wine made her no less alluring to the men around her. They considered her aloof demeanor a challenge to their masculine charms.

*It would be easy, Rat said.*

The woman all in black took another sip of the wine she hardly cared for. Her antintoxicant pills kept the alcohol from affecting her mind. Nothing could cover the taste of the lees, the inferior spirits.

*Easy, she thought. How easy is it to have two simultaneous missions and not know which one will hit first?*

"Just cruise the bars and look as sexy as you can," he had told her. Ratran Yao (who was also Humayun RE4435d, Sinchung Sin, Hroon al-Rashid and many others) stared at her with his blank gambler's stare from behind black dots of eyes. "If any of *his* people see you, they're bound to make a grab for you on the off chance that you *might* be his sister. If they find they've made a mistake, they'll simply kill you. Ramesh Jageshwar employs only the most ruthless and efficient people in his business."

"Not unlike TGO," she had said with little amusement.

Ratran Yao smiled wanly. It hardly counteracted the sad look imparted by his drooping black moustache. Rat, she called him. So did others, but not to his face.

"What about the HRal pair? Why are you interested in them?" she had asked.

"One more time, Janja—while it is every thinking being's right to 'reason why' rather than simply 'to do or die,' it usually does no good to *ask* why. TransGalactic Order wants to find out more about this *linguist,* HReenee. That is all you need to know beyond what we've taught you about her and her brother. Just bring her in. Peaceably, if possible. I've no need, though, to tell you which scheme has the higher priority."

Janjaglaya Wye nodded. Ramesh Jageshwar, so-called king of the slavers, was the current main target of The Gray Organization. And she was the bait, she who had been Janja of "Protected" Aglaya—slave.

She sat now in the Demonhole Bar, dressed in a snug black one-piece. Decorations of silvron grommets revealed tantalizingly minuscule circles of flesh. Buckles of the same material accented her wrists, waist, and ankles. A functional zipper was open almost to her naval, exposing little cleavage of the firm, smallish breasts, yet attracting a disproportionate number of stares.

SpraYon gloves of unrefulgent black covered her hands and arms past her elbows. Laserbeam-thin high heels added fifteen sems to her height and accentuated her powerful calves and thighs when she walked. Her pants gripped those legs as if lovingly.

She attracted stares, certainly, from locals who usually wore simple burnooses cut in the characteristic Fronter style. She *chermed* no emotion other than lust from the men in the crowd, plus envy or curiosity from the women who observed her with furtive glances.

Janja of Aglaya looked human—like a very rare human, true. Yet she was something more than that. Aglayans were not Galactics. Aglayan women could sense the feelings of others, interpret their hidden emotions, detect threats. The ability to *cherm* was not "mindreading" or "telepathy," but it served her well.

This time it alerted her to the presence of a pair of strangers

entering the Demonhole. Not just strange humans, but creatures that thought and *felt* in a manner different from Galactics.

Janja sat quietly, ignoring the men around her. As if
lazily, she watched the two HRal enter the bar with a dozen
miners.

Some of the men around Janja quickly transferred their
interest upon sighting the strange pair. Two pairs of eyes
continued to watch the daughter of Aglaya. They stared
with guarded conniving to measure distances; to size up
options.

HReenee and HRadem *flowed* leggily through the swirl
of smoke, odors, and Galactics toward the bar. Their fellow
miners—eight men and four women—formed a cutting
wedge that enabled them to reach their destination in a few
moments.

"What's the deadliest drink you groundgrabbers serve?"
*Taras Bulba*'s punch-laser handler demanded. He was a
Bleaker who kept the armored glove on his left hand pol-
ished glaringly bright.

"Our deadliest drink?" The bartender wiped at the plassy
surface before her. She was fifty, looked thirty-five and
hard, and had hair as lustrous as dried ink.

"Pos."

She looked the Bleaker up and down. "Cyanide on the
rocks."

The punch-laserist laughed and pounded his armored fist
on the bar. Plasses and pottles bounced for a meter around
the point of impact.

"I like it!" he shouted. "A drink only a Bleaker could
handle! Give me a double. Make it a triple. Grud Scarb's
a hard drinker!" He winked at the bartender and leaned
forward to gaze at her cleavage with eyes that seemed to
want to dive in.

"Make it a mackerbacker, ecstat-eyes. The drink that kills and embalms in one step."

"Mackerbacker it is. How many?"

"Five. I don't know what the others'll be havin'."

The other orders came so fast that the bartender switched them over to the cyberserver while she worked on the mackerbackers.

In less than five mins, all drinks were in hand and the crew of *Taras Bulba* tried to find a table or three. Two rounds of drinks later, the consensus was to stand around until they decided to move on to the next dive.

HReenee sipped at a Pistol Dawn, Front's Premium Lager (it said so on the label). HRadem turned to face a Fronter who'd shouted something.

"Musla," the native said with a blink of his eyes. "I thotchya was a figment—I . . . Musla!"

HRadem smiled through tight lips. His ears edged backward unconsciously. A cyber handed him a drink before he said anything in return.

HReenee gazed around the room, meeting the stares of the other patrons one by one. She saw the startlingly light woman, so dramatic in black. Her felinoprimate pupils narrowed to vertical slits.

During her stay on *Coronet*, Shiganu had told HReenee about the little blond barbarian that had so fobbied Captain Jonuta before his death. (She had only just heard the rumor of a Jonuta lookalike plying the spaceways. She discounted it.)

Curiosity ranked high in the genetic makeup of the HRal of HRalix. She swirled her way past raucous miners and gawking drunks to the minuscule table.

"Looks like we're two strangers here," she said, pulling a chair from under the rump of a man in a tan burnoose who had only just stood. Seeming almost to *flow*, she sat down with it backwards so that she could fold her long, furred arms on the backrest. "I'm HReenee. From planet HRalix."

Over the general noise of the bar, she didn't hear the low growl of an angry male HRal.

"I am Janja. Of Aglaya." *Something's wrong here.*

The pantherish woman took another swallow of her beer and told the blond of her adventures. HReenee had noted the annoying habit of spacefarers to regale barmates with constant updates on their lives. She thought the tradition would be a good icebreaker.

Her fascination with Janja grew when her mention of *Coronet* and Jonuta brought no reaction. And no mention of her ever having heard of the ship or the man.

What she felt next was something more than a prickle of nervous anticipation. Her fur bristled. She grew aware of something reaching deep inside her. Inside her mind. Inside her soul. Something that vaguely searched and probed and *felt*.

Janja was *cherm*ing her, though HReenee didn't know its nature or its source. That she detected it at all would have panicked the Aglayan, had she known.

Four eyes watched the pair of women with more than mere lust.

Near the bar, strong Bleaker hands tried to keep separate a Fronter and a HRal.

Janja tried to sift out the emotions of the crowd from what she *cherm*ed in HReenee and, strangely, more than *cherm*ed. *There is a great danger in this one. Greater than any of the Thingmakers realize. Crippled Galactics, they*–

She looked up at the sound of the scream.

HReenee's ears snapped back to lie almost flat against her head. From the middle finger of either hand appeared a curved claw.

"HRadem!" she shouted, heading for the source of the commotion.

She had hardly risen from Janja's table when the two men jumped them.

# 7

Fanaticism consists in redoubling your efforts when you have forgotten your aim.

—George Santayana

*"HRAAASHAGGH!"*

A furred arm whipped about past the stocky Bleaker. The Fronter reeled back, eyes lacerated by a HRal claw.

HRadem howled again, smelling blood. He yanked the blinded man up from the floor and snarled in his face. His ears lay flat back.

"Furbag, am I?" He shook the whimpering drunk. "Wherrl?" He accompanied his purring inquisition with a look of pure animal malice.

"Don't get fobbied, HRad—" Grud's sentence was cut off by a savage swipe from the HRal.

"Flainin' hell!" The Bleaker jumped back, narrowly avoiding the deadly slash of the talon. It scraped harmlessly across his armored left glove.

HRadem hissed at the Fronter who had insulted him. One swipe tore the crimson-stained kaffey from his head. The man's efforts to soothe the killing pain in his useless eyes resulted only in the bloody leakage of vitreous humors between his fingers.

Daraki watched the events for only a few seconds before touching the control panel in the wide arm of his black lacquered chair.

"'Go of him, you stupid *cat!*" Grud tried once more to stop his crewmate from eviscerating the agonized Fronter. For his troubles he received a backward kick at his kneecap. Had he been from other than a high-gravity planet, the kick might have shattered bone and cartilage.

The stunned Bleaker erupted into anger. Grud drew his chest dagger so quickly that the ornate jewel-work flashed a single streaming trail under the room's lights.

Daraki thought it a prudent moment to act.

Grud brought the dagger down with furious strength toward HRadem's carotid artery (or whatever served as its HRal equivalent) at the same instant that HRadem dug into the Fronter's abdomen.

Grud's knife never connected. A flash of scintillating light an instant before contact gave the Bleaker enough warning. He managed to twist ungracefully and slam into three of his crewmates, scattering them and their drinks into the crowd beyond.

He stood without apology. None was demanded. Anyone would do anything to get out of the way of a stopper set on Fry.

HRadem shimmered for an instant. A howl of rage never escaped his throat, as the molecules that composed his body reduced into atoms and the atoms ionized and scattered. Only a few motes of dust floated next to the writhing form of the Fronter on the barroom floor.

Daraki sighed and switched off the stopper beam that nestled next to the TP camera in the ceiling of his Demon-hole Bar. He regretted the action only because he knew that a killing in his bar would depress business for several days. He sighed again and checked his other monitors.

*Lion of God—not* another *one of them!*

HReenee watched the death of her step-sib HRadem from a few meters away, caught up in her own problems. Though rage and anger threatened to drive her to kill the killer, she managed to avoid HRadem's end. She kicked at the man holding her.

He stood tall and lean, neither of which saved him from the force of her thrust. Crumpling under the influence of a boot in the groin, the copper-skinned man landed eyebrows-first. On the table across from Janja.

The woman from Aglaya struggled barbarically against the grip of a ruby-cloaked man only a few sems taller than she. Her body reacted with the nearly-unconscious speed of her TGO training. A hand snaked about and two fingers jabbed into a nerve juncture under the attacker's arm. His grip instantly loosened on that side.

Before he could react in bewilderment, a laser-thin heel stamped his right instep, followed by an elbow hard and deep in his solar plexus.

"Run!" Janja shouted, climbing over the fallen man.

HReenee jumped past her without even a glance back at the spot where she'd seen her brother die.

By the time her crewmates turned from the bar to look for her, she was outside with Janja.

The street outside the bar possessed all the warmth of a funeral plot. The dust cloud a few light-years out from Front obscured most of the starlight over half the night sky. Garbage and sleeping drunks lined the ill-maintained thoroughfare.

At least it was quiet out here. Janja would not have considered the cliché that it was *too* quiet. No world she'd visited had yet been as quiet as the wet forests of Aglaya. She looked at HReenee, seeing little pain of loss or fear.

"I think it would be best if we went to my room at the Kahafa Round." *Maybe then Rat will let me know the scrute on all this damn' intrigue.* "There we can—"

She stopped in mid-step and crouched.

"There's more of them. Split up!"

HReenee looked about for an instant, not seeing the threat

that Janja seemed to perceive. Her sensitive ears perked to detect the faint sound of footsteps. She had time to wonder.

*How could a Galactic hear that well?*

"There they are," a raspy voice whispered. "But without Carver or Ra'Zutko."

HReenee didn't pause to hear any more. "Kahafa Round," she repeated, and fled into the night.

Janja watched her for only an instant, then turned and ran down the alley that ran parallel to one of Demonhole's walls.

She realized her mistake instantly.

She *cherm*ed the menace lurking in the darkness of the alley, the feeling of a net's being drawn. Then the voice came.

*"Seems 'zif you left before my boys could ask you out."*

He spoke from the shadows, a spill of sickly blue light from a flickering, nearly dead neon sign illuminating the only important part of him—the stopper in his gloved hand.

Janja stood motionless. *Analyze,* the voice of Ratran Yao reminded. *Your opponent is just as worried about staying alive as you are. If he, she, or it is too stupid to worry— it won't care about anything when you're done.*

The stack of crates to this one's right might interfere if she decided to dive toward him. She considered the plan swiftly—and discarded it immediately because it would put her closer to him.

*Assigned to a skungeball planet and about to be grabbed by a flaining slaver all over again. Sunmother, what am I Doing here?*

"We're going on a little trip, cake. I wish I'd caught your friend, too. A pair like you would bring big cred."

Something skittered across the roof to his right.

HReenee's feline eyes adapted to the darkness much faster than Janja's. She saw the danger in the alley as soon as she saw the blond woman run in that direction.

Without waiting to assess the situation, HReenee raced down the street a few meters and jumped up the craggy sandbrick surface of a storefront. The security-obsessed owner had cemented plass (and glass!) shards to the cornices to prevent access to the roof. The HRal found enough width to reach one slender arm over—and pulled.

In one fluid motion, she flipped up and over the cornice to turn in mid-air and land on the rooftop. Absorbing the force of her touchdown with bent legs and a steadying touch of fingers, she ran as silently as possible to the adjacent corner. HReenee insisted on boots with soft rubbron soles.

She looked over the other cornice. And peered directly down at Janja's accoster . . . Janja's captor.

With little thought and a mighty spring of the legs that composed fully half her body length, HReenee threw herself over the jagged edge of the roof. Her clothes fluttered with a gentle wisping sound as she arced through a twisting gainer.

The sound was unusual enough to distract the slaver from his quarry. Looking up, he might have seen the colorful HRal silhouetted against the night sky—if her feet hadn't slammed into his face the instant he looked up.

He made the straining sounds of an amply surprised man and collapsed under her momentum.

"HReenee!" was all Janja could say. She jumped to the felled kidnapper's stopper and seized it.

"It was nothing difficult. We always land on our feet."

HReenee smiled. Her heart pounded and she felt hot even to her own touch. Her thighs tingled. So did other, deeper regions.

The still-conscious slaver had thought that he was as cautious as that famous Captain Jonuta, his ideal. He had taken pain-blockers and Enkephax as a precaution against being knocked out in a fight. Now, breathing dirt and pavement smells, he reached down to his belt and fumbled to pull a release pin.

Swifter than his eyes could register, the HRal disarmed him. Literally.

Her single long claw snapped reflexively out. One quick slash severed the tendons in his wrist (along with veins, nerves and arteries). The same claw slit his throat while her other hand gutted him from navel to sternum.

She hissed in triumph.

Janja stared. *And Ratran Yao wants me to take her home with me ... "peaceably, if possible"!*

With a glance about them, Janja beamed the dying man with the former owner's stopper. The Fry setting tidied up the mess nicely.

The short blond woman felt nothing. The creature had attacked her with a view toward selling her. Now ... the former living, breathing enemy had become a *thing* to be disposed of.

"The hotel's within walking distance. Let's redshift."

# 8

There is the stupidity of the credulous conspiracy-monger, true child of the witch-hunter of yore, who will accuse anyone and everyone on the basis of wild hypothesis and unsupported inference, with no care for the elementary rules of civil courtesy or that famous Commandment which urges that we not bear false witness against our neighbors. This is an old and most murderous kind of stupidity and is the chief destroyer of innocents throughout history.
—Neal Wilgus, *The Illuminoids*

Marekallian's first impression of the *Galactic News* reporter was that she could use a lesson in tact.

"Is it, like, you know, a *sexual* sort of ecstat, ravishing a planet's innocence?"

Eks, sitting in Ahamkara Tsadi's small office in downtown Maniphur, gazed approvingly at her warm topaz-hued skin only partially hidden beneath an aquamarine bando and tights that ran from navel to ankles. Neon beads shimmered in a multi-colored pattern meant to fascinate. The Mindrunner found it irritating.

"Innocence and ignorance are not synonyms, Newser Tsadi. Very few people have any understanding of what the pastoral life comprises. The inhabitants of Protected planets suffer from diseases that don't even have names in Erts. These poor wretches fall victim to smallpox, diphtheria, cancer, plague, venereal disease, influenza, poor eyesight, bad teeth—even *colds!* Everything that a Galactic takes for granted, they are denied. All because of the post-Imperium accords."

Ahamkara Tsadi tapped a stylus against her water-plass and frowned.

"Thed Tyrnyzha personally assigned me to this, so I *naturally* see its newsworthiness. What should I bring with me?"

Eks smiled. "Your TP cam and a few hundred hour's worth of cassettes. And yourself." *And those strong-looking thighs.*

"Where are we going?"

"That would be telling. Just bring something warm."

Ahamkara's nipples tightened beneath her bando, visibly. The neon beads shifted hues.

"How cold will it be?"

Eks stared at her, deadpan. "Ever been to Iceworld?"

She shuddered. "Once."

"Whatever you wore there, bring two."


"Here they come," Geb said, turning to open *Eris*'s airlock for Eks and Tsadi. "This is the stupidest thing he could have done."

Ashtaru shook her head. "He's done stupider." She pulled at her electroblue hair to form angry spikes. A pink swipe of makeup slashed across her face from above the right eye to her left jaw.

"'S'matter, Geb my jacko, never wanted to be a star?"

Geb watched the TP display of the connecting tunnel that linked *Eris* to Lanatia's second-largest orbiting station. He zoomed in on the newser's face. Her Suzite features lent her an air of honesty and trustworthiness. Her deep walnut hair was styled to look full and windblown.

*Typical newser,* he thought. *They're like flainin' clones.*

"Let's go and greet her in the same cordial way we

Mindrunners greet all members of the holo." He sighed and slid off the chair. Looking up at his dayglo-and-ebony crewmate, the midget patted his stopper.

"Dream on," Ashtaru said. "Marek wants her to get the nice-girl treatment."

Geb grinned. "That's your department, Ash my stash. She's not my style."

Ashtaru flipped five and continued to watch the screen.

Ahamkara carried her TP camera headset in hand and the full complement of cassettes in a gray-green insy bag. She scanned the interior of (falsely ID'd) *Eris* with noncommittal smugness.

"Now that we're onboard spacer *Verity*, you can start recording. I know you've seen fancier ones and more heavily armed ships, but this is the finest spacecraft yet devised for the purposes of—" he paused and stared into her eyes— "*Mindrunning.*"

Her big blue (subcutaned) eyes rolled.

Eks drew himself up and cleared his throat in his most no-nonsense manner. "It'll take us a few minutes to unzip from the station, then we'll kick in the drive and redshift."

Ahamkara nodded. She followed him to the con, where he introduced her to the crew. Her first impression (captured on TP) was that Marekallian Eks could use a lesson in taste. The sleek black plasteel interior of *Verity*'s con-cabin contained an unconscionable collection of electronic hardware, medical supplies (most noticeably encephaloboost ampules), and a bewildering overabundance of Universal Edutapes and portable libraries.

"Sorry about the mess. Our holds are filled to the limit. So are most of the crew's quarters. The planet we're heading toward is right on the verge of space travel and we plan to drive a hard bargain."

The newser took one look at Ashtaru and coolly nodded.

*Eris/Verity*'s DS gunner and computrician simply glowered.

"No luggage in the con-cabin," Geb said, not turning his gaze from the bank of telits before him.

Ahamkara looked at the clutter about her in puzzlement. "But I stowed my bags in—"

"You, *seety*." He pronounced the honorific as if it were an insult. "I don't like crowds. Head aft."

The newser glanced from Geb to Ash to Marekallian.

Eks grinned. "Uh—we're a surly but tight-knit group."

"How tight do the nits get?" she asked.

The hatch to the con-cabin slid open. Beyond it stood a sleek, preened figure in platinum and gold. Lights played across the shimmering fur of the Akil. He stood just as tall as the brightly-hued Ashtaru. Nothing but a small saffron breechclout clothed him. Surveying the cabin through his wide golden eyes, he caught sight of Newser Tsadi and smiled.

She stared back. He looked more radiant and beautiful than anyone or anything she had ever seen. From her five-sem advantage in height, she gazed at him and could only mutter an awed:

"What's that?"

"This," the golden stranger said, "is Klyjil bazRakava. I am pleased and honored to meet one of such beauty and poise."

Eks smiled with a sour expression. "Watch out for him, Ahamkara. He's known Erts for a week and already he's a charmer. Plays a mean game of Saberserker, too."

"Where—?"

"You'd be surprised at the people and things a Mind-runner runs into. And so will your viewers *if we could please get under way?*"

Geb grunted and inslotted a SIPACUM cassette. The ship eased away from the space station.

"I'd, uh . . . like to interview all of you over the next few

days. Your views on Mindrunning, anecdotes. *Your* origin."
She gazed directly at the Akil, and a warmth visibly softened
her eyes.

Eks cleared his throat. "I'll be available to you at every
possible moment. And when we're onplanet, it'll be just
the two of us." He detected one of his eyebrows inadvertently rising and stopped it halfway up. "And the Al-fnordi."

"Who?"

"The natives."

Eks could imagine the display running through her mind,
computer-like, as she tried to compare the name to her list
of Protected planets. He grinned. *No sense in letting her
know our real destination. Wagging tongues get arses slung.*

"You'll see," he said, drawing a SIPACUM cassette out
of one of the many pockets of his Panishi khaki jacket. He
removed the previous cassette and inslotted the new one.

*"Abrakadabra.* The work is done."

SIPACUM flashed bright blue telits to acknowledge ini-
tiation of the flight program. The computer also spoke in a
terse, feminine voice that merely said, "Initiated." *"Verity"*
possessed a Computer and Guidance System IV (with Vocally Interactive Computer), which Eks had upgraded sufficiently to rival the experimental Mark VII model.

It had no name, never talked back, and seldom committed
time-wasting (and dangerous!) semantic errors. Eks preferred it that way.

"It'll take a few minutes to find a SPOSE, and then we'll
be on our–" Eks looked up from the SIPACUM console to
see Ahamkara moving toward the Akil.

She adjusted her TP recorder and attached her headset.
An open network of wires, it rested on her head like a tiara.
The glittering black TP camera perched like a jewel at the
center of her forehead.

For a moment, Eks considered asking her not to reveal

the existence of the Akil. He mentally fingerflipped. *It would be a beautiful slap in the face of TGO if the Galaxy knew that a Mindrunner had discovered a new race and TGO hadn't. At least they haven't admitted finding one.* He smiled with sly amusement. *And I know that the Demon Cat won't publicize his Akil.**

The newser approached Klyjil as if she were sneaking up on a grazing zebratige.

"Uh—" She paused, trying to compose her questions.

"Are you as grandiloquent onscreen?" Geb stared up at her with a vicious grin.

She glanced down at the little man without turning her head and TP optic from the Akil. Succinctly she said, "Piss off."

"She's about as polite," Ashtaru whispered to Eks, "as a fart in an airlock."

Marekallian flipped his fingers lightly and whispered back. "She'll serve our purposes. Just look professional."

"Shouldn't be hard, compared to *her.*"


"I don't know where my home world is." Klyjil baz-Rakava stared directly into Ahamkara's blue-subcutaned eyes and looked sadly lost. "I was on a ship that developed engine problems and only barely made it to my lifeboat in time to escape vaporization. I was adrift for weeks before I decided to enter the cryosphere. How long I was there, I cannot say." His eyes widened beyond their normally formidable diameters. "Marekallian suspects I may have been suspended for centuries."

The newser gazed with aching pity into the Akil's mournful golden eyes. His gaze seemed to draw her in. Into his heart. Into his soul.

---

*The woman Kefira. See *Spaceways* #s 5 and 7, *Master of Misfit* and *The Manhuntress*

She shook her head, realized what that must have done to the TP image, and regained her composure.

"Do you find we Galactics to be . . . like, violent and primitive compared to your . . . species?"

The alien smiled with small, beautiful lips. His face resembled that of a lemur only generally. The face of the Akil was so much more lovely that to compare the two would be akin to comparing the face of a Galactic such as Lizina Harith to that of a chimpanzee. Klyjil's beauty was not only in his form, but in his soul.

AhamkaraTsadi felt a stunning infatuation begin to whelm her. She licked her lips with a nervous swiftness. Too, there was the unavoidable thought, the increased excitement: this was an *alien*. Not a Galactic or even a familiar Jarp; not even one of those HRalix-born felinoprimates she had read of, seen in holos, even reported about—and yet never *seen*.

This member of an altogether different race—and definitely a mammalian race!—was *here*, so close . . . and looking at her with those beautiful, soulful, *soft* eyes.

The Akil motioned her closer. She sat across from him on his bed in the medium-sized cabin that had once belonged to Marekallian's brother Denverdarian. The emerald sheets rippled as she slid nervously toward the golden-furred creature.

(*Man,* she mentally corrected herself, *not creature—a man. He is a man from another world—another time, even!*

(*And yet who or what could possibly be more exotic?!*)

"Among my people," he said so very softly, "we have a form of sharing that we call *makhseem*. It is given freely to those who need it. I see that you, Ahamkara, desperately need *makhseem*."

Her eyes moistened. *How beautifully he pronounces my name!*

Trying to maintain composure, she asked, "Do you think

you'll uh find any way to get your—uh—self—uh—back to your—to your–"

A hand of platinum-gold fur caressed her cheek. The tingling that went all through her could not have been only from the touch of soft, soft down. She stared into his eyes. He gazed into hers softly, so softly, so full of . . . gentleness, of feeling.

In one quick motion her hand slid through her hair to remove her TP cam and switch it off.

She caught the downy hand as it hesitantly withdrew because of her movement. She caught it in both hands and pressed those warm, gentle fingers to her bosom.

The headset clattered to the floor beside the bed as Klyjil took her in his slender and deceptively strong arms.

Fully thirty minutes later she was a quivering, twice-spent pool of liquid that somehow murmured a silly, giddy, "I—I've nev–er had so—so much fo–oreplay in my li–ife!"

*"Makhseem,"* her marvelous alien lover murmured, and reminded her anew of his mammalian nature by running his extremely hard and extremely erect Akil organ into her and right up the middle.

She could not even cry out. No, she was not liquid all over; only in the loins. Her vagina was a lake that swallowed his slicer. Her legs and arms snapped around him and adored the soft warm furry feel of him as he began moving, moving, gliding without haste in and out of her.

Eventually he had reason to be nervous, but his careful examination of her proved that he needn't have been. This strange hairless *needing* woman was all right. She had merely passed out from sheer pleasure.

# 9

Before one can identify anything as "gray," one has to know
what is black and what is white. In the field of morality,
this means that one must first identify what is good and
what is evil. And when a man has ascertained that one
alternative is good and the other is evil, he has no justification for choosing a mixture. There can be no justification
for choosing any part of that which one knows to be evil.
In morality, "black" is predominantly the result of attempting to pretend to oneself that one is merely "gray."
          —Ayn Rand, *The Cult of Moral Grayness*

Kalahari Cuw watched the motionless swirls of gray beyond
Roche's Alley and practiced her *Pranayama* breathing. She
sat oncon, unsure about the decision "they" had made to
beam a distress signal at the approaching spacer. An unpleasant disquiet accompanied her decision to assist in the
con-watch for the duration of their repair operations. She
glanced at a computer simulation from the aft TP.

The ship was built for speed and maneuverability. Kalahari Cuw—the former Captain Hellfire—knew what kind
of spacefarer used such ships as that. Slavers. Smugglers.
*Pirates*.

The ship scanned *Sunmother* twice after receiving the *C!*
message. It had approached and cut its engines one klom
away from the yacht. There it had remained, silent and
motionless, for the past hour.

Trafalgar and Quindy worked on the engines. The Jarps slept—Cinnabar would relieve Kalahari in a few more hours according to an eight-and-a-third hour rotating schedule.

*Sunmother* drifted toward Skylla along a rapidly decaying trajectory. Kalahari watched the computer simulation of Skylla's event horizon. A black circle against the gray dust backdrop of the Carnadyne Void. She knew the event horizon—beyond which even light could not escape—and that the mass of the collapstar bent time. If they were not sundered by tidal forces, they would fall forever toward an unapproachable center. Time would slow for them until the universe outside sped toward heat death or implosion . . . unseen and unseeing across the barrier of gravity that was Skylla.

Kalahari shuddered and returned to a normal pattern of breathing. She commed the other ship once more.

"*Sunmother* calling. Are you answering our distress signal? If so, please comm us on this frequency."

The comm remained silent. Then a sudden crackle of static (courtesy of Skylla and Karybdis's rippling waves of synchrotron radiation) caused the very slim woman to jump.

"*Spacer* Sunmother—" The voice was vocoded and impersonal. "*Do you carry any cargo destined for or subsidized by any planetary government?*"

Kalahari frowned. Had a policer managed to intercept them at this moment of defenselessness? And why did the disguised voice neglect to comm an ID? She mulled the question over for a moment, then answered truthfully that they carried no cargo whatsoever.

"*Are you involved in any way with TransGalactic Watch or TransGalactic Order?*"

*Sounds like a flainin' lawyer.*

"*Sunmother* and I are in no way affiliated with any governmental or policing agency," Kalahari said. "Definitely!

The ship is privately owned and in imminent danger. Under—"

The genderless voice interrupted. *"Spacer* Sunmother, *you will be rendered any assistance that you require."*

Kalahari sighed in relief. "Uh, well, for starters . . . could you haul us away from that little dark vortex over there? It looks hungry."

The unidentified spacer switched on a tractor field and towed *Sunmother* back to a zone at the ever-shifting center of mass between the two collapstars. Down in the engine compartment, Quindy and Trafalgar scarcely had time to cheer.

"The left one!" he shouted. "Hit the control rods!"

Quindy swung one long ebon arm and swatted the bundle with her wrist. The polonium rods slid in with a scraping sound.

"Got it."

She crouched below him in the cramped interior of the access tube. They worked in a fury of effort, oblivious to the events outside.

"Hand me the extender." He held out his hand and a tool slapped into it. "Thank you, nurse." He reached for one of an array of nodes barely within his reach.

"Not that one," Quindy said, looking past his body.

"The manual says third from the left."

"Third from *port*. We're upside down. Bridge that one and this whole tube vents."

Trafalgar glanced at the micro-manual adhering to the stanchion a few sems from his nose. "Wonderful. You're right." He slid the extender up to the correct node.

A hiss and grind of metal accompanied the action. It sounded far away through the hull. He listened for a long moment.

"The venting's stopped," he said eventually, "but we've still got to rebuild the damper."

"Maybe our rescuer will help."

Trafalgar flipped his fingers. "Let's humbly beg and find out."

The spacers hard-docked. An umbilical extruded from the mysterious ship to *Sunmother*.

"Locked." Quindy gazed at her crew assembled in front of the airlock. "Stoppers on One. If we've been saved only to be looted, they're in for a fight." She paused and looked at Sweetface. "On the other hand, I don't want any *accidents* if the other crew is trying to help us. Firm?"

All nodded.

"Let's greet our saviours. And see if they can help us get *out* of here!"

Trafalgar smiled. *More like a captain every moment.*

The hatch cycled and slid aside.

Kalahari's eyes opened wide as a Jarp's. As an Akil's.

Trafalgar Cuw grinned his most inviting grin.

She stood with gloved hands on her full hips, gazing with eyes of deep hazel at the crew of *Sunmother*. The achingly white SpraYon gloves stretched from her long hands up past her elbows.

She wore (only just) a tight vest of white polyprop. The hyper-stretchy fabric both covered and failed to conceal the curve of her ribcage and sensual fullness of her breasts. Extraordinarily well-developed nipples were clearly outlined against the sheer vest and and Cinnabar was certain it could see the dark outlines of her areolae through the white opacity. The Jarp kept staring, as if its gaze could make the nipples even more pronounced.

Thin lacing held the vest (almost) together at the front and sides. The ends dangled across her bare midriff. The expanse of naked flesh revealed a smooth, gently curved belly and slender waist that flared into lovely, full hips.

*Hips,* Trafalgar Cuw thought, *that cry out to be grasped.*

Interestingly, Kalahari Cuw was thinking along similar lines.

The stranger's penchant for white continued to the Thebanian wetcloth bit of nothing that circled low on her hips to pass tightly between her thighs. It seemed to serve less as an exercise in modesty than as support for the black spidermesh stockings clinging to her long, muscular legs.

The stockings disappeared into midcalf boots of bone-white equhyde that fitted as snugly as a second skin. The 12-sem spike heels terminated in true, ultra-sharp spikes (tiny suspensor beams in the boot prevented them from punching through the deck or a stray foot—unless that was desired).

Trafalgar smiled and removed his hat to bow with a deep flourish and rustle of blousy yellow sleeve.

The stranger surveyed the crew coolly. Her full lips—colored a deep blood-red—parted in a sardonic smile. Her rich, throaty voice filled the airlock.

"Tura's Towing Service. You called?"

She strode into the tunnel with a swagger that in earlier times would have been called manly. She twitched her head to one side to throw her dark mane behind her.

Kalahari watched, breathtaken.


"Prepare for return to normal space." Geb checked the readouts in eye-bright pink and eye-eez turquoise.

Ahamkara stood to the rear of the con-cabin, recording their arrival. Marekallian Eks stood between her and Klyjil, talking calmly into her mike.

"We're approaching the planet Kabeshunt. It was discovered seventeen years ago by a gem-freighter bound for Franji. The natives are—"

Newser Tsadi groaned and clutched her stomach as *"Verity"* converted from tachyons to ordinary matter. Marek and Ashtaru took deep breaths. Geb quavered a bit, maintaining his position in the captain's chair.

Eks cleared his throat. "The Kabeshunti are a race of saurinoid bipeds on the verge of space travel. They've already sent probes to dozens of stars within a light year of theirs. TransGalactic Order apparently fears that the Kabeshunti might pose an economic threat to Murph. Heavy metal asteroids clutter the system like men around Akima Mars. If these lizard folk start mining them, they'll give us ape descendants a run for our stells."

Ahamkara cast a questioning glance at Eks. "Why do you keep referring to TGO as if they were involved in all this? The post-Imperium planetary accords granting Protected status to planets are enforced by local policers and TGW."

"That—" he held up a finger—"is what the history tapes and TGO would like you to believe. Simply because they have their errand boys do the dirty work doesn't deny the fact that—"

"We've got trouble, Marek." Geb's voice gritted with tension. "Barracuda class patrol ship at eight megakloms. I'm shutting down."

The Mindrunner nodded and turned back to Ahamkara. "Geb is powering the ship down. Modesty forbids me to describe exactly what's happening, but we are about to evade yon TGW cruiser and carry out our mission despite the risks."

Ashtaru kept a steady watch on the Defense Systemry telits, ready to respond if the computers decided to power up DS. Her short cerulean nails scratched lightly at the armrest.

The various spaceship sounds that Ahamkara had become accustomed to ceased one by one. The throbbing of the drive system abated, followed by the gentle hum of the aircon. Even SIPACUM shifted into a silent, low power mode. Lights dimmed almost to blackness.

"We're on passive receptors only." Eks smiled. "The skin of *Verity* is designed to absorb or deflect all frequencies of electromagnetic radiation. The only way we can be detected now is if they happen to see us occult a star. Not too likely, at this distance."

"What now?" The situation prompted the newser to whisper, in spite of Eks's conversational tone.

"We drift like any other chunk of debris." He cocked his head toward his first mate. "Give us some pitch and roll on the gimbals so that we look more like a rock, Geb. On the slim chance that anyone sees us."

Ashtaru called up a simulation from the forward TP. "Cruiser is redshifting Kabeshunt at point nine-five-three."

"Vector?"

"Thirty-three degrees off ours."

Marekallian smiled. "With all the scuz floating around here, we won't be noticed."

"Barracuda class cruiser just hit the Trail."

The captain of *"Verity"* flipped his fingers and looked at Ahamkara with apology. "Sorry I couldn't show you some action. We like nice quiet expeditions."

"Such as the one on Taraba?"

The mention of the Protected planet located far beyond Corsi elicited a smile and a raised eyebrow.

"Ah . . . you've done some research, have you." It wasn't a question.

Tsadi smiled back at him with feral glee. "Actually, I just guessed that might have been you, Marek. TAI lost a ship because of you, didn't they?"

He sighed. "As long as they consider it some sort of crime to elevate primitives out of their squalid condition, I suppose they'll be sending youngsters to their deaths. In the name of 'protecting' planets that neither need nor desire such interference."

"*Interference?*"

"Preventing the free flow of goods and information is much more of an interference in the development of a planet than any supposed cultural contamination, Ham. Regardless of the semantic deception indulged in by the self-proclaimed 'protectors.' There is no reason that any race must develop its own spacefaring ability to become worthy of the spaceways. That's an elitist—"

"I'm cranking engines up to put us on an intercept trajectory with Kabeshunt," Geb blithely interrupted. "ETA forty-seven mins."

He reached up—high—and threw a set of switches. SIPACUM fired thrusters to shift the spacer's attitude.

"Would you like a tour of the medical storeroom?" Marek asked. "It contains the greatest collection of—"

"Actually, I haven't finished my interview with Klyjil." She glanced at the Akil and tried to suppress a smile that was pure pleasure.

Marekallian snorted. His crew exchanged quick nods, returned to their work.

*If she spends the whole flight trysting with that little sweet-talker, I'll have wasted the trip and blown my cover for a holo special on the Akil.* He stared straight at his console, watching the image of Kabeshunt expand.

*Some revolutionary act this'll be!*

# 10

The mice which helplessly find themselves between the cats'
teeth acquire no merit from their enforced sacrifice.
—Mohandas Gandhi

The lobby of the Kahafa Round projected all the warmth
and friendliness of a funeral parlor. An expensive funeral
parlor.

Decorated in early gaud, the exclusive hotel catered to
the uppermost crust of spacefarers and locals. Here Janja
had registered under the name Mel. Jehannam. She'd made
a big show of spending and of frequenting less-than-
fashionable dives.

Whisperers exchanged rumors, opinions, judgments and
condemnations. Mel. Jehannam was obviously a high-priced
hust. No—a rich slut out slumming, looking for kicks.
Perhaps a wealthy, lonely soul, lost and drifting. Her suspected lifestyle revealed the dreams and fears of those who
spoke of her.

She was Mel. Jehannam—and she was watched.

Casual observers in the lobby of the Kahafa Round saw
her, saw the HRal, and whispered.

"Now wouldn't *that* be a sight, the two of them?"

"Looks as if they've already been at it, the way their
clothes are torn. How come *we* never soar like that?"

"You're no cat, Prandar. Stop staring."

86

"Tacky offworlders..."

Janja and HReenee walked through the swirling pastel lobby. The walls displayed shifting holograms of abstract color and depth. Not-quite-discreet little plaques offered the holos for sale at outrageous prices.

HReenee—still trembling from the thrill of battle—quietly observed the surroundings with the offhand attitude of visiting royalty. A couple standing in the lift when she entered stepped deferentially aside. She smiled at her companion.

Janja, visibly shaken by tonight's events, didn't return the gaze.

The hallway of the twelfth floor was just possibly more garish than the lobby. Royal blue velvet (which might have been tasteful if there weren't *so much* of it) combined with prass hardware and tooling to overwhelm the senses. Disguised aircon vents spewed a Fronter version of jasmine. HReenee's nose wrinkled at the scent.

"Stinks, right?" Janja pulled out her passcard and slid it into the door. "I can't stand it either. Smells like rotting meat."

"Good evening," the door said as it dilated.

Janja snorted and walked through. Flopping on an Insarch-sized bed, she let go a nervous sigh.

Hues of emerald and topaz dominated the room. The furniture—antique plass and brass-imitating prasswork—lay about the room in a style that Janja charitably designated "intimate."

The place was cluttered with another age's culture.

She stared at the chlorophyll-green ceiling and said nothing. The room seemed to quake a bit. It rotated and wobbled. Janja utilized her Aglayan ability at psychocytological control. She calmed. The room steadied.

After an uncertain moment, HReenee lay down beside her and stretched. Her fur held the scent of exertion and battle. Perhaps a tinge of blood. It smelled nothing at all like fear.

"I have to call someone." Janja sat up weakly to reach for her tourmaline-hued go-bag. Fingers touched the strap-work of the mindcomm and withdrew it. She excused herself and stepped into the anteroom.

*Ratran?* Janja's silent thought raced through the twisted lines of force permeating the Dark Universe. Somewhere on Front, a matching mindcomm buzzed. And buzzed.

*"Rat?"* This time, she subvocalized the name. It didn't help. A few seconds passed.

Something clicked audibly in her mind and a voice spoke with mechanical courtesy.

*"The one you are calling is unavailable. Please leave a message."*

Janja grinned in spite of her exhaustion. *He's routed the comm through his computer. A damned answering machine!* She still marvelled at the *things* these Galactics loved to tinker with.

"Janja here. I have HReenee in my room. Someone tried to nip us at the Demonhole, but I think it wasn't Jageshwar-related. HRadem was killed in a fight. Comm me."

She removed the straps and brushed a hand through her cloud-white hair. She looked at the HRal woman stretched across her bed.

"Are most of your nights as busy?"

HReenee smiled and rolled over with an unconscious sinuousness to gaze at her host. "No. Yours?"

"Only on weekends." The woman in black sat on the bed and took a deep breath. *"Peaceably, if possible."* Sure. *What's the best way to—*

A soft hand rested on her shoulder. The palm felt hot against her flesh.

*"Whherrl?"* The touch became a languid caressing motion across Janja's aching neck muscles.

"Mmm. Thanks, HReenee." And after a while: "Lower?"

The wonderfully feverish touch of the HRal soothed her. She did not even notice the dried blood still matting the hand's fur. Besides, HReenee's other hand was tracing the outline of her plunging décollètage. The touch was as soft as velvet—yet behind its gentleness was a strength under complete control.

Janja began to feel in control again. In control of her body and emotions, if not of her life. There was something...*odd* about this HRal woman. Not in the way her stroking had become more intense. The oddness was in what Janja *cherm*ed about the HRal.

"I'll be right back." HReenee *pounced* lightly off the bed and ran into the vanitizer. The sonishower hummed quietly at full power for a few seconds.

One shoe dropped, then another. Her *jurl* and reelsilk shirt flitted out from the cubicle and drifted to the carpet in a ripple of purple and blue.

Janja rolled over to stare.

The felinoprimate walked to the bed with a flowing grace born of power and agility. Her long, lean legs moved in smooth, even strides. A fur that was more accurately a soft down covered her nearly everywhere. Her double row of small breasts ran down her torso nearly to her belly.

Something about them reminded Janja of Jonuta. *The prass buttons that ran down his coat!* She smiled. Gone from the spaceways now, that slaver—*her* enslaver—and good riddance.

HReenee paused in front of her for a moment. Janja gazed at the nipples that erupted like tawny little nubbins from the small, even mounds. Her gaze dropped to the shockingly pink, hairless region at the apex of HReenee's legs. The absence of any pubic growth was as startling to Janja as the presence of her own genital hair seemed to most Galactics, who generally depilated themselves from chin to ankles.

Hreenee slid onto the bed. Though she was only a few sems taller than Janja, her slender build and leggy form imparted a tall appearance. Those long legs sensually brushed the large, muscular thighs of a woman raised on a high-gravity planet.

She responded.

To her mild shock, she found that—despite the exhaustion suffusing her—she enjoyed the attentions of the HRal. Fingers stroked and probed beneath her clothing to unseal the molecro bindings.

Slowly HReenee pulled away the other woman's clothing. Its pieces became a black pile at the foot of the bed. Aglayan and HRal lay naked against each other.

A supple hand explored the blond's (only two!) breasts while other fingers lightly touched the recesses of her vulva. They seemed very cool, those inner deeps, to a HRal.

*Mother of MaHRi—she's wet. So very wet!*

Janja's lips sought hers. A cool, pliant tongue insinuated itself and sought out its mate. Her hands ran across small oval buttocks to touch between them. One finger tickled at a coral-pink sphincter while another reached farther and slid into a chamber of feverish heat.

*And I thought her mouth was hot!* She pulled a few strands of her platinum hair away from her face and continued to kiss her volcanic lover.

She felt something prick her backside. She tensed. Without summoning it, her TGO training took control of her actions. A hand whipped about and seized a wrist. In a twisting motion, she brought it up to see. A single claw extruded from the middle finger. A tiny droplet of blood glistened on its tip.

HReenee's small mouth formed an ecstatic grin. Her wrist broke free of Janja's grasp with a savage tug. The HRal's lithe torso slid away. Her long legs wrapped around the smaller woman's waist and locked behind her.

The musky scent of their battle filled the captive's nostrils. Yellow-gold eyes gazed into pale gray. A hand reached toward Janja's left breast, talon exposed. Lightly it traced around her areola—firmly enough almost to hurt, not hard enough to pierce the tender skin.

She watched the naked pink stash rub against her belly. *Mother of Aglii—she's not trying to kill me at all!*

She experimented. Raising her legs, she swiftly jutted them under her captor's arms and thrust back. HReenee fell against the bed.

"HRrm," she groaned.

Janja had no idea that the word was HRal for *yes*. She took the opportunity to push forward and pinion the HRal's arms against the amorphous mattress. At this angle, her pubic mound pressed with firm intensity against the other's groin. The pressure sent waves of delight through her.

All Aglayans of age received ritual circumcision, regardless of gender. There were no frigid women on Aglaya. Janja responded to the insistent contact with increasing desire.

The furred woman below grinned with feral lust and snaked an arm free. Her hand shot up. Fingers raked across the blond's pink cheek.

She gasped, expecting a claw to lacerate her. She felt only a tingle of excitement.

*This is her form of lovemaking! Violent, even frenzied.* She smiled. *Barbaric.*

HReenee raised both legs and brought them together against Janja's ribs. Her fingers reflexively loosened enough to permit escape. In a blur of gymnastic agility, the HRal rolled the two of them over and clamped her thighs against her lover's head.

Her sexual victim struggled briefly, then surrendered to the fiery intensity of her slick, swollen labia and their pressure upon her wanting mouth. A cool, cool tongue probed into her depths. She rolled her hips to rub her clitoris against the upper lip and nose of the face buried in her. All eight of her nipples peeked out from the tops of her lemon-sized breasts. Her partner's two were equally engorged.

Head buried, the Aglayan licked and sipped and stroked. She breathed in the hot, wet scent of sweat and woman-juices. She tasted the incendiary flow from the hot, hot love canal. She couldn't stand it any longer. Shifting around, she made her desire known to HReenee.

After a moment of rearranging, a tongue of fire entered her loins, searching, teasing, reducing her to a hot puddle of sensation. It stroked, tickled and pressed her bared trigger of pleasure. Floating on a sea of sensuality, she tongue-searched every square sem she could reach.

An explosion of delight quaked her body. Her lover twitched in response and stroked her tongue in broad, swift motions against tumescent clitoris and labia.

Janja felt something happening. She soared higher and higher in ecstat. Every time she thought she couldn't soar any higher, she trembled to new heights. Something in her alien lover's body and movement was different from that of any other she'd experienced—Galactic or Jarp.

They flashed together.

In one shuddering, scintillating instant, a thousand waves of emotion/memory/thought washed through Janja. In that instant she knew all about HReenee.

Everything.

Had she any energy left, she'd have sat up in amazement. This was more than *cherm*ing (yet far less than *choncel*ing, for she had not yet drunk the lifejuice of an Aglayan man). She breathed slowly, feeling her feline lover roll aside and make a strange sound. She listened for a moment, in spite of the alarm she felt.

HReenee was *purring!*

She shifted around until she faced the HRal. A kinship

stronger than love bound them now, though HReenee had no idea that her history and that of her people was now Janja's.

*What a secret to bring to the spaceways!* She trembled against the hot, furred body beside her. HReenee, thinking her bed-partner was cold, pulled a corner of blanket over them.

Janja accepted it absently, still replaying the awful truths that she'd learned in their moment of climax.

She knew the true purpose of this supposed "linguist."

She considered the knowledge carefully. *If Rat knew what she was—what she was truly here for—he would have gone after her himself. He wouldn't risk losing—*

Something across the room buzzed insistently.

Janja slid out of bed and strapped on the mindcomm helmet. HReenee watched her with detached interest. Her ears twitched forward as if straining to hear.

*"So you have her. Fine. Bring her with you when you report to your ship. We've got something more important. Big job. You'll love it, Janje. Move it."*

"What if she doesn't want to come along?"

*"Haven't I taught you anything?"*

With that, Ratran Yao commed off.

Janja removed the mindcom and stared at the HRal for a moment. Narrowed eyes met hers. "I–I've got to go now," she said, throwing clothes into her luggage.

HReenee said nothing.

"The room's paid for the next week. I can give you the passcard."

"That won't be necessary. Where are you going?" HReenee sat up, unconscious of her nakedness, and watched her pack.

"Away."

Janja glanced around the room one last time and sealed the two large cases. Picking her black outfit up from the floor, she shook out the RinklFree fabric and slipped it on. She ran a brush through her hair and toweled her face. Slinging her go-bag over her shoulder, she paused long enough to check herself in a mirror and turned to HReenee.

"You'd best forget you'd ever seen me. Forget Jonuta. Forget the spaceways. Go back to HRalix." *That ought to intrigue her.*

She walked to the door and opened it. She turned back to HReenee and struck her most holomelodramatic pose.

"Forget everything, HReenee. Where I'm going is no place for a *linguist.*"

The door sealed shut with a mechanical "Have a pleasant evening."

When Mel. Jehannam departed Kahafa Round in darkness and stealth, a silent figure followed in the shadows.

# 11

I am not an Anarchist in your sense of the word:
your brain is too dense for any known explosive to affect
   it.
I am not an Anarchist in your sense of the word: fancy a
   Policeman let loose on Society!

—Aleister Crowley,
*The Book of Lies*

She crouched in the darkness of Graha's minuscule space-port, watching.

The muscular woman in black walked quickly toward the gray lander. The dust-occluded portion of the sky was no longer overhead at this hour. Crowded stars like scattered gems provided a light brighter than twilight.

Mranophel HReenee sa'fiel rushed from her hiding place toward the ingrav boat. Her soft footfalls barely sounded through the still night air. For an instant she wondered whether the message she'd sent to Captain Darkblood just before leaving Janja's room would get through to the powerful, ardorous Jarp.

She knew that HRadem's death would require a ritual. She made a silent promise to perform it soon. She inhaled the cool, oil-tinged odors of the spaceport. It pulled heat from her fur in soothing waves that matched her gliding steps.

Janja stepped into the lander without looking back. In-

95

stead of sealing the hatchway from inside the airlock, she climbed up to the con-cabin and cycled the lock from there.

HReenee smiled. She had only seconds to reach the hatch and she was nearly a hundred meters away. Her lean, all-muscle legs pounded at the paving, heedless of sound. The last four meters she covered in one mighty leap.

Her body twisted about in midair, slipping between the hatch and the hull with only a few sems to spare. She landed on her feet and absorbed the shock with bending knees. The hatch closed.

"HRrm." She smiled with pleasure and untensed.

*Onboard. Where to? What shall I see and do next?* She fingerflipped with a Shaitan-may-care glee. *Whatever happens, I won't be bored!*

Janja strapped in to the captain's chair and commed Graha Security, requesting clearance to power up. Though she'd failed her qualifying test for spacer captaincy, she was more than proficient at piloting. TGO was TGO; she had her papers.

*"Lander One-Two-Four-Cee, you are cleared for up-powering."*

Clothing rustled. Janja spun her chair to see a bent derelict of a man. Her hand had leaped to her weapon.

He was dressed in a threadbare burnoos and a tattered kaffey, both in drab shades of brown. His hands—old and gnarled—twitched in the helpless manner of nervous degeneration. His gaunt and homely face revealed a wrinkled landscape of veins and sores. The color of his skin varied from sun-damaged walnut to scar-tissue pink.

One sickly, mud-colored eye stared at her while the other jerked spasmodically to the outer corner of its socket. He approached her with one feeble arm extended. His pitiful mouth tried to form words.

Janja did not draw her weapon.

"Hi, Rat," she said easily. "You look slimy as ever. Been cruising the bars?"

She turned from him to throw a series of switches, and tapped instructions into SIPACUM for liftoff.

The man straightened. His entire body shimmered for a moment, than faded. In place of the decrepit oldster stood a figure covered from head to toe in snug pale green. Gloved hands undid the telepresence coif and lowered it.

Ratran Yao gazed wearily from beneath the cowl.

His dark eyes betrayed no emotion. He strapped in and spoke over the roar of acceleration.

"Got her?"

"She followed me from the hotel. I took my time zipping up and she's probably stowed away somewhere."

Yao nodded. "Good. I'll find her later. Lord, you're a sexy piece. Learn anything about her?"

"Not much," Janja lied. Every skill she possessed of body-and-mind control she channeled into concealing her new knowledge. To reveal it would be to reveal the depth to which she was able to cherm the HRal.

That was something she intended to tell no one. TGO was TGO—and Janja was Janja.

She said, "When her step-sib got poofed, we had too much action to do much talking."

"How about at the hotel, from the time you left the message to when I commed you?"

"Uh–" Janja hesitated.

The broad-shouldered, deceptively thin man smiled. The ends of his drooping moustache twitched lightly, satirically.

"Cat got your tongue, Janje?"

Janja merely gave him a look. Inwardly, she thanked Sunmother that he questioned her no further.

"I'm accompanying you on your next assignment. We've

received a communication from the *Iceworld Connection* about some big trouble. You're going to be part of an ultra-wet wet job."

"What is it?"

She spoke without facing him. Her gaze remained divided between the telits and the field of stars beyond the viewing port. His mention of the Iceworld Connection merely reminded her that he would not tell her what it meant.

"Oh, all in good time." Ratran Yao stretched back in the chair and yawned. "When we dock with *Light of Aglii*, you'll plot a course for Murph. More accurately, for the sixth planet orbiting Aristarkos. It's owned by TMS Mining Company, same as Murph. It's an uninhabited, frozen, nearly airless world."

"What's it called?"

"It has a beautiful name—Kebri Dahir."

When they docked with Janja's sleek, more-than-beautiful TGO spacer, she programmed SIPACUM to plot a course for Kebri Dahir.


Surdiakah—Master Strategist for the Council of Ninety-Three—watched computer simulations of battle plans for the Carnadyne Horde.

The Horde consisted of forty-three Orca-class dreadnoughts, built near Redoubt. From there—amid the sparse reaches between two far-flung spiral arms of the Galaxy—crews had transported the spacers to the murky, dust-strewn expanse called the Carnadyne Void.

One hundred twenty-eight support spacers waited in the Void with the heavily-armed battleships. Freighters, repair craft, scout ships...all attended the Horde. Their crews (both human and cyber) would not return to the spaceways until the Council had provided the Final Solution to TGO and its uniformed branch, TGW. The human workers had agreed to such conditions by contract.

The cybers, of course, had no choice.

Surdiakah ran through a battle plan involving concerted attacks on TGW's three known headquarters. Based on information from reconnaissance and leaks, the computer estimated DS strength and spacer readiness.

He discarded the plan after cycling through several hours of the attack in accelerated time. Any of the three bases could repel a direct assault with minimal damage. The Horde was still too small for that.

Surdiakah smiled with a sardonic memory of holodramas in which a handful of warriors in a rag-tag fleet would assault an incomparably larger foe and win. *How many fleas*, he mused, *have ever taken down a gamelephant?*

*If that flea can* infect *the gamelephant, though ...*

The Master Strategist's long arms bent back to stretch. *Marekallian's right, in one sense. This is indisputably a public relations game. We've got to convince the planets to stand with us against TGO. But to do that, we need the Horde. Mindrunning won't help us a bit.*

*Except for the treasures dear Marek brings us to fence.*

Surdiakah keyed up another battle plan, knowing full well that in actual combat confusion reigned supreme. Computer simulations could not yet duplicate the vagaries of the human mind. His understanding of this had assisted his rise to the position of Master Strategist.

Surdiakah had not been wrong yet.

The "yet" haunted him, as he supposed it haunted everyone. The possibility of failure grew with every emboldened move that the Council made. Activity attracted scrutiny. The inevitability of espionage turned Surdiakah into a private, guarded man.

Though only a few of the most loyal council members

actually possessed navcassettes bearing the location of the Council Redoubt where they were now assembled, any conspiracy with more than four or five people was invariably known and infiltrated by the very people being conspired against.

Surdiakah knew this and accepted the unavoidable probability that TGO knew the general nature of the Council and its plans. He reached for his cup of HyperCaf and downed the last swallow.

*There's only one thing that makes victory possible.* He stared at the computer screen for a long moment. *No individual or group can know everything about another individual or group. Hidden factors—that's what makes space races!*

In this case, the hidden factors were the people the Council hoped to impress. He reprogrammed the computer to run his own plan. He postulated that no one particularly cared for TGO and TGW (or TAI and local policers, for that matter!). Even though most people would acknowledge that TransGalactic Order had prevented war for generations, nobody liked to *pay* for its upkeep, nor did many people see a need for TGW and TAI. Neither seemed able to rid the spaceways of piracy or slavery.

Besides, who liked policers, anyway?

The battle plan played out before him in accelerated time. The Carnadyne Horde attacked not as a fleet, but as tight units. Simultaneously. At a dozen targets. They attacked TGW outposts in as many star-systems, crippling spacers and disrupting communications.

The simulation demonstrated that surprise attacks on local garrisons yielded an eighty per cent success probability.

*Then the ships will comm a message to the liberated systems that they have been freed from TGW interference, taxes, and controls.* He tapped a few ruby-hued keys and watched the dispersion of orange light points on the screen.

*Support personnel orbit the inhabited planets and handle public information. They coordinate recruitment of volunteers for additional attacks on TGW bases. The dreadnoughts are already on their way to the next dozen garrisons.*

Thus would the resistance spread. *An infection started by a fleabite.* Surdiakah massaged the back of his longish neck and smiled. *No—it's an innoculation administered by a tiny injection that creates antibodies to restore the system to health!* He smiled.

*Good semantics make a good revolution!*

The door to the simulation room opened. Surdiakah's wife Drushallah quietly entered. She wore a red and gold Franjisari and carried a tray with a carafe of Bose and two plasses.

With a smile and ceremonial bow, she filled the two plasses and handed Surdiakah one. Though she was a tall woman, beside her husband she appeared to be of ordinary height.

Drushallah placed the tray on the console beside her husband and silently picked up her plass. Surdiakah nodded with affection and smiled with appreciation at the unexpected refreshment. He took a deep sip and savored the flavor.

At that instant Drushallah, Surdiakah's wife, ran into the computer room.

"The Reshan ambassador!" she cried in breathless frenzy. "He's been found poison—"

Drushallah looked at herself serving her husband and screamed.

Surdiakah looked from one Drushallah to another. His hand instantly shot forward to reach for the comm-mike. Fingers faltered and clenched in agony. Rising halfway out of his chair, he struggled to focus his dying eyes on the alarm button. The poison brought him to nervous degeneration in seconds.

Master Strategist Surdiakah fell to the floor, twitched once, and fell into an irreversible coma.

The woman in the aurasuit set down her plass gently and flicked her wrist at Drushallah.

Something hit Drushallah's red and gold Franjisari above her left breast with a *snick*ing sound. Surdiakah's wife looked down to see and feel a thin, feathered needle sticking through her sari into her flesh.

Her holoprojection double picked up the plass (still full) and walked over to grasp her in one arm. She trickled a small amount of the poisoned Bose into Drushallah's mouth. A firm hand stroked at her throat to guarantee that some of the poison reached her stomach. Just enough to make it look like a suicide pact.

She withdrew the paralyzing dart from Drushallah and reloaded it in her wrist launcher.

Behind her, the comm switched on to feed information to Surdiakah. A tangle of voices crowded each other in an attempt to relay information.

*"—financiers from Jorinne are dead—all of them!"*

*"—at the planning session, dozens of them. Dazed, amnesiac. BRAINWIPED!"*

*"—said something to me about the Horde and just dropped dead right there!"*

The aurasuit's holoproj shimmered for a moment as the woman inside straightened up and switched miniholocassettes. Suddenly she was Surdiakah. Not quite as tall as the Master Strategist, but no one would notice or care, under the circumstances.

Surdiakah ran into the corridor, joining in the general confusion and compounding it with contradictory orders.

The Master Strategist directed medical crews to empty

rooms and commandeered emergency carts—parking them in the middle of panicked crowds.

"There!" Surdiakah shouted to a pair of frightened guards. "Beam those insurgents!"

The guards nervously covered the crowd with number Two beams, causing the mob to dance in a frenzied rictus of jangled nerves and confused motor functions. When the guards turned around to receive further instructions, their Franjese leader had vanished.

On the space station's observation deck, people rushing to their ships encountered a devastating spectacle. One by one, the dozen or so ships clustered around the station vanished into thin vacuum. No sound (of course); no light, no motion. As if they had been plucked from the universe by an angry god.

Actually, it was worse than that. They had been snatched by a dispassionate TGO.

The Council of Ninety-Three (minus forty or more) was stranded in deep space. Thousands of light-years from any known inhabited world.

In the death and chaos, no one noticed a figure wearing a flat-black spacesuit exit from an auxiliary airlock and kick off into deep space. The tall woman who had been both Drushalla and Surdiakah drifted for several minutes.

When she had placed a few hundred meters between her and the station, she pressed a series of studs on the wrist of her mlss.

The survivors at the Council Redoubt concentrated on removing and identifying the dead and sending distress signals via upper-limit tachyon beam. Terrified and confused, they failed to search for an imperceptible figure's shielded ion thruster accelerating her toward an equally dark spacer a thousand kloms away.

The trip would take several hours. After she boarded,

she would take two days' R&R, then set course for Tera-saki—and a Visit. Linked to the spacer's SIPACUM by light-beam laser, Valustriana See, TGO, took the opportunity to sleep.

As soundly as a baby.

# 12

I have no confidence in the kinds of contrived situations
that a certain school of analysts is so fond of. Real war does
not resemble a game of master-level chess...
   In a real battle, confusion reigns, communication is difficult, if not impossible, and clear thinking is obscured by
terror and agony.

                              —Admiral Noel Gayler (USN Ret.)


"Killer ships?" Janja's face became a mask to all emotion.
She stared at the man, her eyes the color of frozen hydrogen.

"Three of them." Ratran Yao leaned forward in his chair
just enough to look earnest. The movement accentuated his
thin features. "You'll be piloting one of them, Janja. It's
got a standard Yuan con-cabin, with high-response DS and
missile targeting computers. Handles like a jinni. You'll
love."

*Another killing* thing *made by the* thing*makers*. "Why
should I enjoy that, Rat?"

"Because, my darling little berserker, you're a moral
avenger in a universe annoyingly short on clearcut black-
and-white choices."

SIPACUM *ping*ged three times. Still wearing that satiric
smile, he glanced at the con to see the cause. A small
collapstar in their path necessitated their return to "normal"
space. The conversion from tachyons to ordinary matter
caused as much discomfort as usual.

When the spacer and its contents returned once again to the Tachyon Trail, Yao continued.

"What we have here is a clear black-and-white division. One of the few you'll ever encounter." He leaned forward a few sems more—so close that he smelled her womanly scent. "The Iceworld Connection has information about a fleet that's been assembled in the Carnadyne Void."

*(She must have known about it for months,* he thought with bitterness, *and just didn't think it important enough to mention. And she had to get back to one of her damned experiments before I could get a location out of her!* Damn you, Carnadyne!)

*(Still . . .)*

Carnadyne—the woman, not the Void—never ceased to mystify Ratran Yao. She had been a he before he/she went Forty Percent City. She had beaten the odds, returned from the Dark Universe. But . . . not completely.

She still existed in some thoroughly untidy and eerie fashion in both universes. Simultaneously. To watch her (if one could overlook her stunning, malformed ugliness) was to watch a being that seemed to flicker in and out of reality at the edges. Parts of her extruded in and out of the Dark Universe.

She had turned an insane curse into a goddesslike benefit.

She was Carnadyne, and she saw things that no other human had or could. She even saw the Carnadyne Horde.

And couldn't be bothered with it!

Ratran Yao had difficulty understanding Carnadyne's priorities. She could spend weeks examining the rate of evolution of a Crozite vent microbe and nearly forget to rescue people that she had sent into peril.*

Nearly—but never completely.

Janja was looking at him, waiting. "The Void is a pretty

---

*As in Spaceways #11, *The Iceworld Connection*

vast place to hide in, Rat. Did this Iceworld Connection give you a precise location?"

"Leads, nothing more. It ties in with a set of SIPACUM cassettes we tried to confiscate on Sekhar some months ago. One agent died and another is temporarily using TPs for eyes thanks—I suspect—to a Mindrunner named Marekallian Eks."

"Mindrunner?"

"Sort of a smuggler. This one sells technology and information to natives of Protected planets. Then he loots them. Nice business, right, Janja? Get the natives dependent on Galactic technology. Then, while they aren't looking, plunder what little wealth they possess. Almost as kind as slavery. Except that a slaver affects only those he enslaves. A Mindrunner desires to infect an entire *culture.*"

Janja shuddered. "And the Iceworld Connection has found these Mindrunners in the Carnadyne Void?"

Ratran Yao fingerflipped. "Uncertain. Something big and nasty is brewing there, though." He tapped a few keys on the console and called up a location check: any mass radiating infrared in the range of 39 to 40 degrees centigrade.

"Our stowaway's in the equipment bay. Probably asleep. I think it's time for me to 'discover' her."

"What do you want to know from her?" Janja hid the tension rising in her.

Ratran flipped his fingers casually. "You know. In—for—mation. By hook or by crook."

"She's got her own hooks, crook."

Ratran Yao smiled and rose from the chair. "I've already noticed your little cuts, snowcap. I plan to be a bit more careful."

"Freeze in a cold hell, Rat."

"Doubtless," he muttered, and winked, and redshifted the con-cabin.

The slender man walked down the tunnel with slow, light

steps. The light "gravity" imparted by axial rotation decreased markedly as he approached the core of the spacer.

The equipment bay contained the majority of heavy machinery and replacement parts for *Light of Aglii*. Located along the central axis in order to minimize the energy needed to spin the ship, the equipment bay consisted of a maze of containers and bins lashed to the bulkheads against the accelerations, decelerations and weightless conditions of the spaceship.

As with most storage areas (even on a ship as new as *Light of Aglii*), the air inside assaulted the nostrils with scents of oil, ozone, dust, and corrosion. He noticed not at all, creeping quietly toward the plasteel crate where the TP scanners had pinpointed HReenee's body heat. The sound of gentle breathing reached his ears. Gazing over the edge of the man-high crate, he saw the rise and fall of HReenee's lean torso. He reached out and lightly tapped her thigh.

A hand whipped out from its resting place under her head and snatched Yao's wrist. Just as quickly, he twisted it away in one smooth motion and brought it down hard against one of her small warheads. She gasped in pain and surprise.

"Stowaway, uh?" He grasped her left arm and pulled.

Her middle finger silently exposed a claw and dragged it across the flesh just past his wrist.

At the first impulse of pain, he rotated his arm and applied crushing pressure to her radius and ulna (or their HRal equivalents). With one strong pull, he dragged her off the crate and flung her to the other side of the aisle.

She floated effortlessly in the low-G, writhed about, and kicked off from the braces of the opposite bin.

"Mind telling me what you're doing up here?" he demanded, not taking his gaze off her even to check his arm for damage.

She shot back at him, both talons out. He easily side-stepped and jabbed straight fingers into the nerve bundles of the brachial plexus under both her shoulders.

Before she hit the wall without the braking power of her paralyzed arms, he grabbed her legs and pulled her to a stop.

Just the touch of her body and its feverish heat sent an electric surge through him. He quashed the impulse.

He pulled her close to lock her long, downy legs with his. That kept them from kicking. She exuded the scent of a woman in passionate heat.

*Maybe I'm just using it as an excuse,* he thought, *or maybe she really* is *soaring on this.*

He pulled her head back and gave her throat a savage bite. Not enough to break the skin—just enough to elicit a low, purring moan from the HRal woman.

Slowly she regained the use of her fingers. The claws had retracted by reflex. Now she grasped his buttocks and brought his loins closer to hers. One long-fingered hand snaked into his tights and tugged them toward his knees.

She left the rest up to him.


Ahamkara Tsadi gazed at the lush turquoise and creamy pinks of Kabeshunt's surface in hushed awe. The turquoise oceans contained hues of blue, green, aquamarine, sapphire, and emerald. The pink land masses varied from nearly red at the equator to sandy white at the poles. The landscape was a random spread of scarlet and pink and peach and rose. On the limb of the planet, the atmosphere formed a tourmaline crescent across the daylit hemisphere.

Her pupils dilated as if to take in more of the view. She turned at the sound of someone entering.

"Nice chunk of real estate, hmm?"

Marekallian Eks joined her at the viewing port, just for a moment, and glanced out. His fingers tapped commands to SIPACUM on the con keyboard.

"It doesn't, you know, *look* like it's colder than Ice-world."

Eks grinned. "Well, maybe the summers are a bit milder." He flipped his fingers and resumed entering commands.

"Keep an eye on the central land mass as we approach, Ham. It looks uninhabited now, but wait until the visual resolution increases. The planet's packed with cities. Population's about eight billion. They've got small settlements on the three moons and several orbiting stations. What they don't have is double-p drives or tachyon converters. Guess what they'll have by the time I'm done."

Ahamkara switched on her TP camera. "They don't sound like they're suffering down there. Why do you want to upset their Protected status?" Her deep blue eyes strove mightily to achieve a penetrating gaze.

"If they *were* suffering down there—as many are on other Protected planets—what possible moral justification could there be for preventing me from bringing the benefits of technology to them? And since they *aren't* suffering, they obviously won't be a drain on any other planet's resources. Either way, there's no reason that any planet should be quarantined from free and voluntary contact."

"A backward people would be prime targets for exploitation," she said, and thought, *Chew on that one*.

"Who's more exploited—an azaafrunn picker on Alachi or a miner on Murph? One planet is Protected. The other isn't. And how exploited is un-Protected HRalix compared to Protected Aglaya? I haven't heard of slavers grabbing a HRal as a choice sport."

"You're twisting words about."

"Word-twisting is a newser's business. My most sincere apologies for bettering you at it." He bowed deeply, came up grinning. "Take a look at the planet now."

She swallowed the rising anger of arrogance, and looked. She saw the unmistakeable signs of civilization on the planet ahead. Straight lines connected square and round clusters. Cities, canals, surfaceways.

"We won't be landing. There's an orbiting manufacturing center where we'll dock and meet with the Kabeshunti there."

Tsadi shook her deep walnut-hued hair and frowned. She steadied her camera before asking, "When you meet them, you'll just hand over a drive and a converter?"

"Working models and detailed plans, actually. I'm not made of cred, you know." He smiled with as much boyish innocence as he could muster.

"How can you afford the ship and supplies? Are you demanding payment from the natives?"

His smile remained plastered on. "It's very important that what I tell you next not be edited in any way or taken out of context. Agreed? I know a fugitive can't protest his treatment on the holo, but my own TP is running oncon for a complete version."

"I'll run this segment straight. As I would anything else," she hastily added.

"Good." He held up a finger. "One. The consortium of manufacturers and capital accumulators to whom I'm delivering these items is paying for them. Freely. Eagerly." Another finger shot up. "Two. I don't believe in altruism, and the psychological profit I derive from Mindrunning won't keep my operation going for long. I don't run a charity ship. Three." He stared directly into her TP camera.

"I suspect there will be a sudden increase in amateur Mindrunning when I tell you that the price I'm getting for the drive and the converter is roughly equal to a tenth of Kabeshunt's gross planetary product.

"I'm not robbing anyone and neither are the buyers. It's their money and the merchandise is my property. All I'm doing is breaking a law—an artificial barrier to trade. And I'm making a flaining fortune from it!" His smile enlarged into a grin.

"So you're dragging a planet onto the spaceways for profit."

"Damn' firm! I have my money and the Kabeshunti have the stars. Nothing is damaged except the reputation of TGO and TGW. That's the way life should be."

Ahamkara Tsadi gazed at Eks, silent for a moment. Her forehead displayed an uncommon frown.

*Let her mull that one over.*

"We're a thousand kloms above the orbit of the station. I've had SIPACUM beam an ID to them and they've responded. Docking time is esti—"

SIPACUM buzzed twice and overrode *"Verity"*'s comm. A message appeared on the screen in screaming orange letters on a black background.

*"Gri's grick!"* He read the message a second time, unwilling to believe it.

Ahamkara jockied about to get a TP picture of the screen. A firm hand shoved her away face first.

"Sorry, *seety*. We've got a problem." His fingers punched keys rapidly. He swung the comm-mike up to mouth level.

"Geb! Blueshift oncon and chop it! Ash! Unzip from Phoenix and set the cargo capsule to jettison." He spoke without turning to Tsadi. "Either get to your cabin or strap in back there. We're blowing this dirtball."

"You're—you're what?"

"We're redshi—"

"What the vug?" Geb careened through the con-cabin hatchway, caromed off the DS chair and pulled himself into the first mate's chair.

"Redoubt's been hit, Geb. It's been hit hard. They sent a *C!* by scrambled tach."

"But everyone was there. That—" He stared up at Eks. "Drishna's cock—that means . . ."

"Damn!" Eks shouted, pounding the console's keys with swift, angry fingers. "Damn it *all*, I didn't want this!"

Geb took a deep breath and tried to control his trembling. "That puts you in command of the Carnadyne Horde!"

Eks shook his head. "No. I didn't want it. It won't—"

"What's the Carnadyne Horde?"

"Shut up, ass!" Geb reached for his stopper.

"Jet it, Geb. Program a course for the Horde by the fastest repeat *fastest* route."

"Right, boss." Geb slipped a SIPACUM cassette into his keyboard slot and added a few commands to the information already coded into the crysplas card.

"You," Eks said to the newser, "can keep quiet. We're in great danger courtesy of TGO and I won't entertain any questions. Ash!"

*"In the cargo bay, Marek."*

"Attach a beacon to the cargo and jettison it. We're redshifting—now."

*"Firm."*

"What about your profit?"

Eks turned furiously to face a smiling Tsadi. She reclined in her chair—strapped in—and watched him with her TP camera still on.

"To hell with it! If TGO gets me tomorrow, at least I'll have one last strike against 'em! Geb—status!"

The first mate pulled the cassette from his keyboard and slotted it into SIPACUM. "Ready."

Eks addressed SIPACUM's mike. "Find SPOSE and enter with ten sec warning. Enter program *Typhon*. Get it?"

"Got it," replied the quick, soft voice of the CAGSVIC. "Good."

*"Cargo jetted,"* Ashtaru reported.

"Firm. Now we wait for a SPOSE." The Mindrunner let go a sigh and stared at the beautifully mottled planet. It drifted from view as the spacer came about, rotating.

Ashtaru rushed into the cabin, a stopper holstered on either thigh. She tossed Geb his plasma beamer.

Eks eyed the transfer. "Let's not go overboard. We're just running to the Horde."

"If they found Redoubt," Geb said, "they've got to know where the Horde is."

"Maybe. Maybe not."

"What do you plan to do with the ships?"

Eks smile was one of weary wistfulness. "I haven't really decided, yet . . ."

# 13

Out of the mud grows the spaceship.

—Booda

The trouble with retirement is that it knocks all the fun out of holidays.

—Kalahari Cuw

"Will this help?"

Trafalgar Cuw took the proffered chipboard from Tura ak Saiping and looked it over. "Should work." He handed it down to Quindy. "We'd be better off with a quanta damper, though."

"Had I only known," Tura said, "I'd certainly have had a spare ship in tow."

She watched the pair working with mild disdain. *Help a stranded spacer and waste a flainin' day*. She took a drag from a stick of redjoy and smiled.

Quindy—sheathed in a jonquil jumper that matched her hair and did nothing else nice for her—grunted under the main console. "I need a bus."

Tura leaned down. "Which one?"

"Uh—8901100-LLP40. And a forty-one."

"Not much problem there. I'll scare them up." Tura turned to go. "Anything else?"

Quindy chuckled. "Sure. A TDP or two."

"Right."

115

Trafalgar's eyes widened and he raised an eyebrow at the Saipese ship-master. "Just happen to have a few anti-glitchers lying around?"

She gave him an overly cool look. "As a matter of fact, Cuw-ball, yes I have. And I'd be glad to give one to your Captain Quindarissa. Any objections?"

Trafalgar gave her an overly sweet smile. "None at all, Cap'm Tura."

Her face continued cool and low-lidded. Appraising, maybe. "Think you can shove one over from *Black Dawn?*"

He pushed back his hat and looked at her. He made it a cool, appraising look. No trouble; Trafalgar Cuw knew how to use his face.

It seemed to him that beneath the taut vest her nipples tautened under his gaze, which grew interested. Her full lips formed a sensuous smile without quite parting.

*Haughty*, Trafalgar Cuw thought. *Self-assured. Challenging. Bet she just can't help it.* He stood to meet her eye to eye.

Her hands rested on her svelte hips with SpraYon-coated fingertips tapping against her holsters. The nails looked long and sharp. Her eyes stared, and now he thought that she was *working* to maintain that cool look. Her nostrils flared with each breath.

He said, "I can shove anything you want wherever you want it."

She nodded toward the umbilical that connected the two spacecraft. "You make good talk. Let's see you walk."

"Captain?" he asked in Quindy's direction.

The captain of *Sunmother* hesitated for a moment. "Pos, go with her and get the equipment, Traf. I can work on other parts of the system."

"Firm."

She listened to them drift out of the con-cabin. She felt curiously unconcerned. *She's interested in him. Wants him.*

*Of course—who can resist Trafalgar? And if he enjoys her, so what? He'll be back.*

She touched an ebon hand to her sweaty forehead and returned to work. *Sunmother and my life are the two things that I control. If I have to use Traf as a hust to save them both—why sure, I'll do it.*

Knowing it didn't make her feel any better.

The Kabeshunti monitored the approach of the Galactic spacer with hearty anticipation. One of the saurinoprimates, an emerald-hued nesting-male named N'Agk Sheshregk, watched the docking computer calculate *Eris*'s approach to the orbital station.

N'Agk Sheshregk adjusted the gain control on the monitor to improve the picture. The tiny soft scales on his three fingers rasped lightly against the dial. The opposable thumb protruding from just above the base of his palm turned the control gently, adjusting while he stared at it with yellow eyes.

Soft yellow light bathed the control chamber. It imparted a damp sheen to Sheshregk's body. In the warmth of the space station, he wore nothing but his toolbelt and food bandolier.

An intricately detailed bronze device hung from the pliant ornihide belt—his only weapon. It looked like a set of brass knuckles with three fingerholes rather than four. A simple but bewildering series of studs controlled the hidden array of blades, spikes and hooks that made up the ceremonial weapon of the Kabeshunti.

Sheshregk had never drawn it in anger. He was not the sort. Nesting-males, after all, required patience and an even temper.

That good humor began to fade when he saw *Eris* turn tail and redshift.

"Alert!" he called in a voice that rasped like claws against granite. "Craft departing! Find the reason!"

He towered over the others with his 210-sem height,* which was not uncommon for a nesting-male. Especially for one who had chosen a career in space.

"Craft has ejected a small mass." That from a claw-female whose red and yellow scales gleamed from rigorous (and time-consuming!) buffing. A fine chain-mail breech-cover concealed her egg-cleft with modest totality. "It is radiating a message impulse in the Mindrunner's language. Interpretation on line Seven."

Sheshregk called up the translation on his screen. It indicated that the crates contained two devices—the ones the alien had promised them.

*He does not remain to receive the balance of what we have agreed to pay him.* The nesting-male tapped his jaws together in mild agitation. His lines of small teeth clacked lightly. *Is he generous, forgetful, or deceptive?*

The stakes for the near-spacefaring Kabeshunti were high enough that Sheshregk hesitated no longer.

"Bring it onboard. Alert the analysts to prepare for study and report."

The reptilian biped leaned back in his soft conformal chair and took in a breath. He could smell the woman to his left without resorting to the obvious (and *rude*) means of extending his slender blue-black tongue for a better olfactory sample. She smelled delightful. Perhaps this triumph would impress her. Perhaps she would permit him into her nest.

N'Agk Sheshregk shook his head happily. Things were looking up for him. Almost as an afterthought, he felt pride in the knowledge that things were also looking up for his species. The Mindrunner was dead right, of course. The

---

210 centimeters: almost 6 *feet*, 11 *inches*, Old Style.

Galactics did not own the stars and the star-worlds and the great gulf between!

Onboard *Black Dawn*, Tura ak-Saiping and Trafalgar drifted through the ship's hold. Unable not to watch and admire her easy litheness and the rounded beauty of her bottom, Trafalgar Cuw was not thinking of an extremely expensive Anti-puterglitch device from Sekhar.

"Here. Have a TDP," she said, turning sinuously in air.

Casually she handed him the ridiculously costly component. Her onyx hair drifted about her head in the null G. Her breasts floated high on her chest, seeming to strain against the white fabric of her tightly-cinched vest as if they wanted to fly right off.

"How much do you want for it, Captain Tura? We're not carrying any cargo, but we've got some cred—"

The formidable Tura fingerflipped. "Not necessary. I've seldom seen a new spacer in worse condition."

"You're an honorable spacefarer, Tura."

Trafalgar spoke with honest feeling. He didn't bother mentioning the TGW inventory stickers he'd noticed on the bottom of the device and the two busboards he held.

"Honor," she said with a breathy laugh, "toward those who merit it." She floated idly, regarding him.

His tight-fitting crimson work jumper terminated in a pair of prassy metallex boots that reached halfway up his calves. Good body on the man, she thought. No—a great body. Almost as fine as Ranta—

"Follow me," she said, almost impulsively. Hand over hand, she pulled toward the hatch and into the tunnel.

He fingerflipped and followed her out, one hand holding the precious electronics while the other worked with his feet to pull and steady him.

She led him up to a hatch surfaced with black lacquer-look pressed plas. On it were several rows of gleaming prass studs like ancient rivets.

"Nice door. Keep a dragon behind it?"

"In a sense. Want to come into my dungeon?

Her breath quickened and her eyelids lowered just enough so that she had to tilt back her head to gaze at him.

*Imperious bitch, isn't she Traf m' boy?* He nodded toward the hatch. "Open up and let's see."

The hatch cycled. She had programmed in a deliciously low creak and grind. She gestured him inside. Trafalgar graciously bowed and entered.

Yellow-orange lights flickered on imitation torches mounted along the walls. Walls that looked as if they had been cut from stone. Gray walls.

Trafalgar's eyes were a few seconds adjusting to the low level of light. Then he saw the equipment.

"This is my exercise parlor." The hatch sealed shut behind them. "Like it?"

*Now, what's on her mind?*

He gazed at the X-shaped wooden cross on one wall. Black equhyde straps floated from various points along it. Near another wall stood a low set of stocks, complete with an ancient, rusty padlock. On the third wall rested what Trafalgar Cuw presumed to be her "exercise" equipment.

The basic tools of torture had varied only slightly in design throughout history. The physics of pain dictated a uniform design. Manacles, straps, ropes to restrain the victim. Whips and crops to lash the flesh. Clips and pincers to apply pressure or worse to select points. Blunt, long objects to probe and penetrate.

Tura ak Saiping had all these instruments in their primitive forms. No lectrowhips, no janglers, no slavetubes. Just an egregious quantity of equhyde and leather, prass studs and steel spikes.

Tura, all in white, looked like a sensuous angel until she

picked up a meter-long steel rod with a leg-cuff on either end. She nodded toward a low, cushioned imitation altar against the fourth wall.

"Spread your legs, worm." She floated over to him, staring with cold, aloof cruelty in her eyes. "You want to taste the passion that I can unleash. I see it in your hungry eyes."

Trafalgar smiled easily.

"No thanks. The only thing I'm hungry for is a square meal. I'll be heading back to *Sunmother* now." He pulled himself around and cycled the hatch. "Thanks for the stuff."

"Stop, you coward!" Her voice practically snarled. "Men would give their slicers to bend in worship of my stash. Under my lash you'll learn the—"

"Theba's icy erozone, you sound like one of those semi-literate ads in a compuTryst. Can't you see—you've mis-read me. I don't go for that shit, *Domina*. See . . . it's more blessed to give than to receive. I *give,* lady."

He kicked out of the chamber and maneuvered away.

Tura ak Saiping floated quietly in her dungeon.

Her thoughts returned to the man she had lost a year before. Murdered, as she thought, by TGO. It had changed her. She had become what she was now by choice. New name, new face, new goal. *Do I even have a new soul?*

None of it would bring Randy back. It all added up to reaction, compensation, vengeance.

She let the manacles drift from her grasp. Picking out a whip, she cracked it furiously. Reaction sent her twisty-floating.

*Bastard*.

Something moved in the corner of her vision. She kicked herself around.

In the hatchway floated a slim, taut woman. Her gray skinTite bodysuit was snugger than skin to neck, ankles and wrists. Scrim shoes and a thin gray velvon belt provided the only accents. Long fingers sported short, unpainted nails. Her dark hair was short and unstylish; her figure angular.

Tura gazed into the woman's eyes for a long moment. In the low light of the chamber, they smoldered with turbulent emotions. *She,* Tura thought, *is involved in one big fat decision!*

"Kalahari," she said, still holding her whip, "you just missed your brother on his way out."

Kalahari Cuw—related to Trafalgar Cuw only by virtue of the forged document he had procured for her—pushed into the "exercise parlor" and sealed the hatch after her.

"Whatever you want from me," she said breathlessly, with a strange determination, "I'll give you."

Tura stroked the braided equhyde of her whip and smiled. *"Give? Me?* You can't give me anything, girl. I take! Come and lie down. I'll ease your hurt."

"Would—could you call me Quindy?"

"I'll call you what I want to, Quindy, you wicked nasty punishment-deserving bitch!"

The whip lashed with a savage crack.


"Here's a gift from our rescuer." Trafalgar handed the TDP to Quindy. "TGO property."

"Um. So?"

He flipped his fingers. "So she's probably a pirate. So my sensibilities are easily shocked." He reached in to palm and press her left warhead. Automatically she put back her shoulder. "How soon till we're unfobbied?"

The black woman sighed and ran a hand across her yellow-subcutaned hair. "With these, about an hour."

"Make it two hours and take off your clothes, wench."

She raised a querying eyebrow.

"Sorry," he said. *"Captain* wench, then."

Quindy chuckled. "Tura didn't take it all out of you?"

He took hold of her chin roughly and held it there while

he kissed her just as roughly. His tongue plowed into her mouth as an invader rather than a gentle lovemaker. His other hand grasped her breast again, roughly this time. Her eyes were flaring and she was panting when he released her.

He unsealed his worksuit, watching the revelation of her breasts and lower torso as she too undressed.

"I didn't offer it," he said. *Not on her terms*. He reached. "I love these things, did I ever happen to mention that?"

"A time or two. Uh! E–easy . . ."

"No."

With a great shudder, she grasped at his firming penis while his fingers gave her the rough "rapist" treatment she always wanted, because she needed it.

"I love this thing, did I ever tell you that?" Her voice was low, very soft.

"A time or two. Talk, talk, talk. Show me."

That slicer was thickening and firming in her hand. "Here's an offer I won't let you refuse," she murmured, and her head moved forward to him.

Her lips enshrouded him, to his groaning delight.

# 14

You can't say civilization isn't advancing: in every war, they kill you in a new way.

—Will Rogers

TMS Mining Company either considered Kebri Dahir worthless, or simply had not gotten around to cutting it apart yet. Janja ordered SIPACUM to guide the spacer toward the gray, airless world. With a tired sigh she actuated the autoplanetfall mechanism.

"Touchdown in two hours." The voice of her CAGSVIC IV spoke in a calm, precise tone that soothed her.

"Thank you, Saladin. Is Ratran on his way to the con?"

"Pos."

"In fact," a voice from the rear of the cabin said, "he's here." He wore a NueSkin patch on one wrist and an exercise outfit of beige tights and loose saffron shirt.

"I warned you about the claws."

Yao stared with blank, implacable eyes. "Use these co-ordinates." He placed a cassette in her hand, which she inslotted without comment.

"You're withdrawn," he said.

"There's a difference between withdrawal and reticence." She brushed a few strands of lightly-gilded white hair away from her eyes and concentrated on the computer simulation of their descent.

"You're having doubts about what you're doing in TGO.

124

You're wondering why you're staying. You think—look at me. All right, don't. You think this is just another kind of killing. You're transparent as plas, Janja of Aglaya. I can read you like a glowing screen."

"I'm always thinking those things. There's more, Rat." *More about HReenee and the future of Galactics than any of your race will find out!*

He flipped his fingers. "Secrets are my business. I find out what I need, sooner or later. For now, be as reticent as you want while I tell you a little story."

"A story of good against evil?" Her sarcasm was level, lifeless.

"You know better, though as I told you earlier—this is as close as you'll come, as I told you earlier. White and black you left behind when you departed Aglaya—if it was ever there, either."

"I didn't depart, I was *enslaved.*"

"And you killed your slaver. Sub'nalla. How many people does a slaver affect? A few hundred? A few thousand, max? We deal with the big ones, Janja."

He leaned closer to her shoulder, watching with her the simulation of their descent.

"We'll be heading for the Carnadyne Void by fastest possible route. The fleet hiding there consists of more than forty Orca-class battleships. More firepower than has ever been assembled. More than double the number of ships Artisune Muzuni possessed, with five times the firepower. Whoever's assembled this fleet can only intend war. So we disperse it, Janja. The hard way."

"We kill them."

"We stop a few thousand aggressors before millions of lives are lost. We've already accepted that killing is a Bad Thing. Large numbers of dead people are worse than small numbers, unless you think *any* killing is bad. If you do, you have a poor personal record of pacifism."

Janja nodded, eyes closed. "Firm, firm, firm, and pos. Damn you, Ratran Yao, you know that I'll pilot your damned killer ship and I'll kill for what I think is right. It's just that nothing seems right if I think about it for too long."

*Nothing to look forward to but more slaughter.*

Janja gazed at the spacer through the viewplate of her mlss and felt a thrill course through her, despite her disquiet. She followed Ratran's yellow mlss as they sortabounced across the gray, dusty wasteland in the .47G gravity of Kebri Dahir. Above her, the sky was purplish from the density of stars nearby.

One portion of the sky was a dull, dark red. The Carnadyne Void.

To her right, HReenee paced a meter away, wearing a bright red mlss. Janja's own pressure suit shimmered a deep green under the light of the star Aristarkos.

"Welcome along, HReenee," Janja commed without much enthusiasm. It was the first time she had seen her since they'd parted at the Kahafa Round.

"HRrm." HReenee replied absently with her language's affirmative. She was staring at the ship Yao was leading them to. "I do not think following you was a wise decision. You are far more complicated than I'd thought. This is no place for a linguist."

*Fear? From her? Or does she know what Rat wants from her?*

Janja kept pace with the long-legged HRal by virtue of stronger legs bred in high gravity. She knew Rat was listening to every word. She presumed HReenee knew it, too. That seemed unimportant. Rat had in HReenee a far from unwilling captive.

Janja would never tell her TGO superior that his wanting the HRal fitted right in with HReenee's plans.

At first, only the vertical prow of the killer ship poked

above the rim of a small, ugly hill. The trio rounded the gentle curve of a cliff eroded by eons of meteorite strikes. Janja gazed at the spacer and gasped in spite of herself.

It stood only seventy meters from stern to prow—smaller and sleeker than the spacecraft in which she had hunted and killed Kislar Jonuta. Yao had assured her that its engines provided even greater thrust and its weapons comprised far deadlier power.

Face invisible behind the reflective helmet, Yao gazed with pride. One tap of a stud on his left glove signaled the airlock hatch to cycle open.

He bowed in mock ceremony and waved the women onboard.

Even in her pressure suit, he noted HReenee *flowed* with a noble grace that was at once inspiring and arousing.

Janja moved with her own brand of voluptuous strength. If he'd had any time to ponder the concept of a *menage*, he might have watched them more closely. They were on the hunt, though, and time was everything.

Onboard and unsuited, he steered his very sexy companions into the con-cabin.

Janja noted that it was indeed the standard Yuan configuration, with a few additions such as DS and SIPACUM panels within easier reach of the master's chair. One person could oversee maneuvering and placidation simultaneously. (In a culture that referred to killing as "placidating" or "Poofing," DS—Defense Systemry—was a natural euphemism for weapons that tended to attack as often as to defend. Or oftener.)

Yao punched up a holo of the spacer's main weapon. "Ship's DS uses a high-speed, semantically cognitive VIC to control a devastatingly accurate missile system."

"Missiles?" Janja frowned. "When did TGO take the great leap backward?"

He replied with deadpan languor. "Missiles as small as

these are almost undetectable, Janja. Even if a computer caught one coming at an Orca, it would identify it as a pyrocket or some other insignificant piece of ordnance. It doesn't emit any radiation because it's not a nuclear weapon—as if that would ever be allowed."

He smiled sanguinely, remembering the pleasure he had taken from personally eliminating Vilarik and his "safe" nuclear research facility from the spaceways.*

HReenee cleared her throat in a polite, curious manner. Ratran continued to address Janja.

"The cyprium armor of an Orca would ordinarily resist anything that could be thrown at it. However—" He tapped at the computer simulation of the missile's marble-sized warhead. "Inside that little bauble is one gram of anti-matter held in magnetic suspension. When it hits the hull, the field collapses and the anti-matter makes contact with any matter nearby."

"Photons," Janja said without lifting her gaze from the screen.

"A ridiculous amount of them, according to al-Einstein. Enough to punch through cyprium and tear quite a hole through the spacer. Each of the three ships is equipped with one hundred missiles. We'll be concentrating on the dreadnoughts. The other ships we'll spare so that the crews can escape with their own rumors. Think of this as a public relations effort."

*This is war*, the Aglayan thought. *War to prevent war, war without civilian casualties, war with risk to minimal personnel—but war all the same.* She sighed. *At least there will be no possibility of killing any innocent parties. We're guilty on both sides.*

HReenee cleared her throat again. "May I ask why I am being made privy to this information? This seems to be an

*Spaceways #9, *In Quest of Qalara*

internal dispute among Galactics without a need for anything amounting to an outside observer." Her ears flicked forward quizzically, as if straining to catch each word.

The man who was called Cougar and Sin Yanshin and Humayan and Ratran shifted his attention to the HRal. His emotionless black eyes gazed thoughtfully into hers of yellow-gold.

"I've been interested in you for some time. When we have a free moment, I'll explain what I want from you. Right now, though, just consider yourself a part of the team. You see, I know how your encounter with Menekris ended."*

HReenee stiffened. "Does TransGalactic Order normally increase its membership by *conscription?*" She pronounced the last word as if it were Shaitan's first name.

"No," he said with a deadpan expression. "We'd rather *impress* you." He turned back to the con and inslotted a cassette to SIPACUM. "Captain Janja, you are oncon. Take us to the Carnadyne Void at maximum velocity."

"Firm. Crew zip up and prepare to redshift."

She powered up the engines. They sounded startlingly near in the small spacer.

HReenee watched Janja with dawning realization. *She did not meet me by accident. I was baited and drawn. And the Rat caught* me! While she did not appreciate the turned tables, she was still where she wanted to be. Regardless of her voiced hesitancies, this was where she wanted to be.

She eased into the chair behind Janja's and strapped in.

Yao sat to Janja's right. Within a few minutes, the crush of acceleration was behind them. At two megakloms from Kebri Dahir, the ship shifted attitude a few degrees. SIPACUM calculated a Safe Point Of "Subspace" Entry and flashed its turquoise telits four times. SPOSE. A pleasant bell sounded a warning.

---

*Spaceways #6

"One minute," the ship's Vocally Interactive Computer said.

"Do you have an operating name?" Janja asked.

"Farkash, *seety.*" Its voice was masculine, soothing, trustworthy.

"Are you interfaced with DS, Farkash?"

"Yes, *seety.*"

*So polite! And hardly the voice one would expect a battle computer to have.* She wondered why a battle computer should have any type of voice in particular. *An anthropomorphism,* she thought, and gave the concept no more attention.

"Tachyon conversion in ten seconds," Farkash advised.

Janja braced herself. The conversion from ordinary matter to tachyons scrambled her nervous system enough to bring on nausea and headaches. Some lucky few spacefarers never experienced any side-effects. They were in the extreme minority. Some few others may have taken one flight wide awake and vowed never again to be sensate on the Tachyon Trail.

Between those two extremes lay most spacefarers. The range from mild discomfort to vicious headaches, vomiting, release of bowels and bladder, and fainting comprised the most familiar reactions to tachyon conversion.

"Rat," Janja asked. "What happens to the anti-matter when we convert? Does it become anti-tachyons?"

He flipped five and showed a satirical half-smile. "Good question. How would anti-tachyons behave? Maybe it's the same as with photons—no matter–antimatter characteristics. All I know is that we haul them around without any problems."

He said nothing more, turning his head to watch the rich field of gem-studded space before him. Almost directly ahead lay the dark swirls of the vast, rocky dust cloud.

Janja felt her head swim in disorientation. HReenee

growled a HRal curse. Ratran Yao did nothing, made no sound. His thoughts were somewhere deep within the Carnadyne Void.

Janja wondered what the other two were doing, caught herself, and forced her attention back to the con. *I don't care if they're slicing each other from here to Harb and back again.*

The trouble was, she did care. Her hatred for Ratran Yao was balanced by their enormous mutual sexual attraction. He had kidnapped her and tricked her, saved her and given her a purpose. He had granted her wish—to end Jonuta's life.

That he was recruiting a new agent should not fill her with doubts and questions. Yet it did.

*What am I to him? Another tool to serve The Gray Organization? Another shadow in its phantom order? If I die tomorrow, will he go on?* She knew the answer to that one, and it filled her with a sort of pride. Pride in Ratran Yao. Pride in her man.

The thought jarred her. *My man?* She shook the thought away. Absurd. She had no love for Galactics, for the *thingmakers.* She was worthy of Aglaya and they were not.

*If only I could find a man of Aglaya. Oh, Tarkij! Have I strayed so far from the path of Sunmother? For one taste of your lifejuice would I give all . . .*

SIPACUM's bell rang gently. "Collapstar ahead," Farkash said without concern. "Converting to normal matter."

Janja took a deep breath, let it out slowly.

The spacer dropped into "normal" space, maneuvered around the area of frighteningly compressed mass, and returned on its course toward the Void.

"Captain Janja." The VIC spoke with clear inflection and no trace of accent.

HReenee spoke in much the same way, Janja realized.

The result of learning an alien language. Learning it exceptionally well.

"Yes, Farkash?"

"The destination you have specified can be reached within the time limit stated by means of only one course."

"That's true."

"By maneuvering between the collapstars Skylla and Karybdis."

"Pos, Farkash. Having second thoughts?"

"Neg, Captain. However, I note that you plan to maneuver through Roche's Alley using manual, real-time trajectory corrections."

"So?" She knew what the computer was courteously attempting to tell her.

"SIPACUM is perfectly capable of calculating and maintaining a safe, high-velocity trajectory through such a narrow corridor. This particular spacer is capable of passing within a few megakloms of the event horizon of either collapstar without a serious shift in direction. We are low-massed with high thrust engines. I–"

"Farkash, I understand and agree with all you've said." She ran her fingers through her short, pale hair and smiled. "A friend of mine once boasted that she had negotiated the Skylla-Karybdis Roche's Alley five times. Supposedly a record. I'd like to try it once. A captain should."

The computer said nothing for a moment. When it spoke, its semantically cognitive circuits had already digested and understood Janja's implications.

"Your friend reads as being an excellent pilot and ship-handler. Will–"

Janja interrupted. "Give me a simulation."

"Simulation," Farkash acknowledged.

Onscreen appeared two black dots, mere points that were almost parallel and well separated. Each was surrounded by a simulated blue corona. Around that blue ring appeared another, in red. The color-added simulation filled the screen, the red circles overlapping.

Janja nodded; the black points represented Karybdis and Skylla, each a collapsed star. While tiny in cosmic terms, each contained a fantastically compressed mass. When the stars died and compacted eons ago, they had become unbelievably powerful sources of gravitational pull. Each blue corona represented a collapstar's Blue Event Horizon; anything passing within that blue-marked range (at no matter what velocity) would be caught and dragged into the collapstar. Each red circle indicated the decreasing gradient of attraction. Within those circles (actually spheres, in space), a moving object would not *necessarily* be dragged in.

The higher the initial velocity of a moving object, the closer it could approach the blue circle and still be certain of escape. With a radically altered trajectory, perhaps. The immutable laws of relativistic physics provided easily calculable velocities and distances.

Too close or too slow, and any object—including a starship under power—would be pulled beyond the Blue Event Horizon. No amount of thrust could break it free, then. It would be an ensnared fly, dragged helplessly into the clutches of a lurking, ravening spider—the collapsed star that was neither black nor a hole.

Shooting past a collapstar usually required nothing more than a minor course correction. Maneuvering between *two* collapstars was a dangerous—usually fatal—sport.

Everything in space moved. Nothing was still. The collapstars Skylla and Karybdis, separated by only a light year, orbited slowly about a common center of gravity. Other such pairs existed, here and there in the Galaxy.

This pair, though, was in the Carnadyne Void, and that made all the difference.

Their insatiable gravitational appetites cleared the Void of debris between the two centers of inconceivable mass.

That made the passage seductively attractive to spacefarers eager to trim a few days travel-time from their trips. The constantly changing orientation of that clear channel, though, made it a deadly trap for careless, impatient ship-handlers.

The red circles overlapped. Had the blue circles done so, passage between Skylla and Karybdis would have been impossible. In fact, if their event horizons so much as touched, the two collapstars would rapidly—and calamitously—become one. As long as they remained in a stable orbit, it was possible—however risky—to pass between them.

Roche's Limit was the minimum distance to which a large satellite could approach its primary without being torn apart by tidal forces. The mathematical limit applied primarily to planetoids and close binary stars.

The first Galactic to discover the clear channel between Skylla and Karybdis was much more familiar with Bussard ramjets, however, than with the fine points of astronomical theory. He had called the ever-shifting passage Roche's Alley, and the name had stuck.

"Correct," Janja said. "This is our course. Right up the Alley."

"Acknowledged," Farkash said equably; reluctance had not been built into its voice. "The excellent ship-handler of a friend you mentioned—will it be entering the Great Race?"

"I don't want to talk about her, firm?" She felt the tears that welled in her eyes.

"Firm." Farkash silently returned to guiding the ship through the emptiness toward Skylla and Karybdis.

# 15

Security is mostly a superstition. It does not exist in nature,
nor do the children of men as a whole experience it. Avoiding danger is no safer in the long run than outright exposure.
Life is either a daring adventure, or nothing.
                                              —Helen Keller

When war is declared, Truth is the first casualty.
                                              —Arthur Ponsonby

Farkash alerted Janja to the presence of the two spacers at
a distance of nearly four hundred megakloms. To port
(somewhere) lay the ravenous collapstar, or "black hole,"
called Skylla. To starboard, another: Karybdis. The pair of
slow-moving spacecraft lay ahead off the port bow.

"We must decelerate, seety." The VIC was as courteous
as ever. "At our present velocity, our relativistic mass in this
narrow corridor could perturb the other ships' trajectories.
Sufficient perturbation could propel them toward Skylla's
event horizon."

"Or drag them away. Can you calculate probabilities?"

"Pos. However, I cannot predict how the captains or
computers of the other spacers will react."

"Show me," Janja said.

"Simulation," Farkash acknowledged.

Onscreen appeared the overlapping red circles surrounding the blue circles that in turn surrounded the black dots that were Skylla and Karybdis.

"Blow it up," Janja said. "I don't need the outer arcs of the red coronas, I need to see the ships. All three. Compress the scale if you have t–"

A double explosion roiled over the screen, expanding.

"Oh *blast*! Someone left holes in your programming— Farkash! By 'blow it up' I meant enlarge the image, not, uh, blow it up. Needs to be made bigger so the ships will be visible as more than the tiniest of points, firm?"

"Firm. You have remarked the lapse in my programming. Shall I program myself to respond to the command 'blow it up' by enlarging the image?"

Janja considered, without patience, while her ship covered more thousands of kloms. *Some "semantically cognitive" computer* you *are.* "Later. Remind me. Right now, damn it all, enlarge image and–"

She broke off, since the command had been given and the image appeared before she could restate it. She studied the screen.

Here came Janja, from due "south," just approaching the "bottom" of the red circles, where their overlap formed a double loop. Above, well within the leftward red corona but definitely not in the blue and thus lost, were displayed two other objects. Orange squares.

"My ship is the arrowhead configuration—that is, the green isosceles triangle. Why are the other two squares?"

"The triangle is a vector indicating the ship's direction of movement and magnitude of thrust. As neither of the other craft is in motion with relation to the two collapstars, I have not shown a direction of movement. Would you like vectors indicating their freefall ballistic trajectories?"

"No no. Very good. I see the problem. Damn! There goes my dream of cruising up the Alley . . ."

She sighed, watching the triangular simulation moving steadily and knowing she was watching the passing of thousands and thousands of kloms.

"Decelerate to a safe velocity," she ordered. "Stand by on DS. They may be our other two killer ships. Maybe not. Scan all wavelength and tach-beams for messages."

"Firm. Standing by."

The ship yawed about to use its engines as braking rockets. The con-cabin hatch slid open within seconds. Ratran entered, followed by HReenee. The pair of light tan exercise tights he wore revealed every muscle on his tight, hard body. HReenee wore just a little more than she preferred to wear onboard a spacer (nothing)—a pair of loose, burgundy colored trunks.

"What are they doing there?" he asked, gazing at the vague computer simulation of the distant spacers.

"Sightseeing," Janja said.

"Neutrino flux indicates they may be involved in repairs. One point source is intermittent. The other is functioning at low power. Just enough to keep it from drifting toward the singularity." Farkash paused. "I can now simulate spacer configurations."

The vague images tightened up into familiar shapes. The configurations read out below the orange simulations in yellow characters. Farkash repeated the information aloud.

Janja stared at the screen. The smaller ship looked sleek and powerful. Not much larger than this ship, it was either a rich Galactic's plaything or the property of a smuggler. Or a pirate. The other ship . . .

Janja's vision swam. The other craft was *hers! Sunmother!*

HReenee noticed the way Janja stared at the con. Her ears twitched back. *Something is creeping through the little one's mind.*

*What do I do, Sunmother? Do I stop to aid my friends? They're part of the past I've tried so hard to leave behind. No matter that I love them all dearly.*

Janja bowed her head, tried to think. Rat would never allow a delay in their journey. He would forbid her to contact the spacer if he knew what it was. She looked edgewise at him. *He knows almost everything about me. He'd know that's* Sunmother *if he's paying attention to the simulation.*

The thought suddenly struck her. *What if it's all a test? False scrute fed to the computer?* Casually, her fingers tapped at the keyboard, running a parity test on the sensor input versus the screen's output. It firmed. What the screen displayed matched what lay scores of megakloms ahead.

*Please, Aglii. Prevent me from having to* choose. *Let us pass without—*

"Receiving a message," Farkash said.

The commbox crackled into service. *"Hoy, approaching spacer. We can barely get a reading on you. We're in need of a quantum oscillation damper. Please comm us."*

Janja trembled at the sound of Quindy's voice.

*"I see that you're decelerating. Are you planning to render assistance? Please reply."*

The owner of *Sunmother* bit at her lower lip to combat agony with pain.

"Are we down to safe velocity, Farkash?" Her voice revealed only a sad efficiency.

"Yes, Captain."

"Cut engines, rotate, and set course along the following geodesic."

She read off a string of numbers from her own calculations. The course would use the gravity well of Karybdis as a sling to throw the ship out of Roche's Alley and onward to the first octant of the Carnadyne Void.

*"Spacer—"* Quindy's voice held disappointment. *"You*

*are not on an intersect course. We are willing to pay for a damper, if you have one. Please reply."*

Leaving the comm silent, Captain Janjaglaya of The Gray Organization continued on her mission. The pain knifing through her heart was the only grief she permitted.

"Whoever it was," Cinnabar said, "it sure didn't want to hang around here."

"Neither do we, jacko." Trafalgar tossed the Jarp a handful of computer chips. The crysplas pieces flew every which way in null-G. "These don't work. Add 'em to the Satana Coalition's vast stores of wealth."

Cinnabar retrieved them and threw them into the nearest disposall.

Quindy looked up from the con. "We'll get out of here without their help."

Cuw closed the access hatch to the main computer. His smile was pure pride. "We'll get out of here now, if you want, Cap'm. Everything is online and unfobbied."

Quindy sighed. "Great! Has anyone seen Kalahari?"

"Not lately," Cinnabar said. "Should I comm her?"

"Don't bother." Kalahari's voice carried in from the corridor.

Quindy waited a moment for her to enter. Hearing the sounds of her redshifting the con, the ebony woman pushed out into the corridor.

"Kala—?" She stared at her former captain and lover, speechless.

Cinnabar and Trafalgar joined her in the tunnel, and joined her in gaping.

None of them stared at the light bruises along Kalahari's arms and thighs, nor at the dried stains on her clothing. Her three crewmates stared at Kalahari's hair. It was short. Not just shorter than she usually wore it; her hair was whacked off. And it was white. White as the top of a cloud, with just a hint of gold.

All were surprised. Trafalgar reacted first.

"Mmm-*hmm*," he muttered. He moved about to view her from all sides.

She looked at the Outreacher with enough surliness to indicate just what she thought of such scrutiny. She started to say something, stopped short.

"Poor sister Kali—" Trafalgar said. "You're afflicted with some intimations of sentiment despite yourself. Is our friend Tura a psychiatryster?"

*"Why don't you put a cold-patch on that noisy hole in your face!"*

She grasped a standpipe and flexed her arm. The tug pulled her away from the trio with surprising speed. In silence they watched her maneuver through the tunnel toward her cabin.

She turned a corner, missed the handgrab, and bounced off the tunnel wall.

"Flainin' damn' sisterhumpers!" She regained her direction and disappeared from view.

"Poor little slunk..." Trafalgar shook his head, and the former Captain Hellfire would not have believed the emotion, the empathy on his face.

Quindy had already returned to the con. Fingers darker than midnight roamed over the SIPACUM keyboard. She said nothing. Cinnabar sat in the navigator's chair and threw a bare orange leg over one of the padded arms.

*Poor Hellfire,* it thought. *Always looking for something never quite within her grasp. Janja left us and doesn't want to be found. She could be ten thousand parsecs away from us. Why hope to find someone in a universe so vast?*

While it mused upon human frailties, Sweetface entered the cabin, reminding Cinnabar that a Jarp had as many frailties. It greeted Sweetface with a gesture of camaraderie.

"Hello, Cinnabar," it said in Erts.

Cinnabar replied in the whistling tongue of Jarpi. "Dammit, Sweetface, turn off your dam' translator!"

They both laughed. Cinnabar, whose translator was an expensive implant, reached up and lightly turned the switch on Sweetface's translahelm. They spoke in whistles, gestures, and motions of their large, round eyes.

"I wish we weren't leaving just yet." Cinnabar smiled wistfully. "I'd like to give that big Saipese a workout."

"T'lee," the other Jarp agreed, without too much enthusiasm. Since losing its love partner Tweedle-dee to slavers on Front, Sweetface was given to long periods of morose introspection. "She looks like a bruiser, though. Did you see those marks on Hellfire?" It used Kalahari's former name whenever the two Jarps conversed in their own tongue.

"T'lee. They were pretty light, though. A lot of fantasy, I'll bet."

"That Turaloo's a pirate. Traf told me as much. *Sunmother*'s been repaired with stolen TGW equipment."

Cinnabar made Sweetface a gesture of amusement. "Think I care what a sexy *narrow-eye* does to those flainers?" It watched Quindy run a thorough systems check.

Sweetface watched, too. "Cinnabar . . . think they'll ever really accept Jarps?"

"Think they'll ever accept themselves? They can't stop enslaving each other." The unhelmeted Jarp gestured freedom. "The Satana Coalition isn't enslaving us. To them we're comrades, friends, lovers, crewmates. What more are you asking?"

Sweetface replied so slowly that its whistle was almost inaudible. "Understanding."

Cinnabar put a six-fingered hand on the shoulder of its friend. "That," it said, "they do not even grant to themselves."

It stood and stretched. Touching the subcutaneous micro-

switch with its tongue, Cinnabar spoke to Quindy in fluent
Erts.

"Shall I tell Tura ak Saiping that we're ready to cast
off?"

"Thanks," she said, "but I can comm her just as—"

"It's really no trouble at all."

Captain Quindarissa ran a fingernail down the side of
her jaw and grinned. "You have twenty minutes while I
cycle through the final check. Don't come back in a bag."
*Did I just say that?*

"Firm, Seety!" It winked at Sweetface on the way out.

It winked back. Cinnabar's enthusiasm for sex improved
Sweetface's disposition a few notches. *Nothing wrong with
Cinnabar,* it thought, *that slicing or being sliced won't cure.*

*There it is!*

The instant SIPACUM detected the Carnadyne Horde,
Marekallian Eks cut power to the double-P engines and
switched on the comm. Beyond the viewing port of the con-
cabin, only a ruddy darkness surrounded *Eris*. Though vis-
ibility in this portion of the Carnadyne Void reached for a
megaklom or more, they were more than twice that far from
the Horde when ship's sensors at last detected the fleet
through the debris.

Alone oncon, Eks swung the comm-mike toward his
face. *"Eris* to *Liberator*—request security clearance on code
*TYPHON."*

While he awaited their reply, he switched on the spacer's
interior TP monitors. Ahamkara stood at an observation port
a few levels back, recording everything.

*Fine,* he mused. *You'll get a light brainwipe before I
return you to Lanatia. Plus a seamless editing job on your
cassettes.* He zoomed in on her shapely legs and crawled
the image slowly up past her hips, waist and pushy bustline

THE CARNADYNE HORDE 143

to her lovely face. *And maybe a mild encephaloboost to convince you of the importance of my mission.*

*And to improve your grammar!*

"Liberator *to Eris. What is your purpose in coming here? No inbound flights are sched–*"

"I am arriving under code *TYPHON* repeat *TYPHON*. The Void has blocked you from receiving information regarding the attack on Redoubt. Captain Kukavi will firm the code. What are you, a cyber?"

There followed a long pause. *No doubt walking on his hands to three superiors before getting through to Kukavi. Damned insidious burok. Why can't people take action!*

*"Uh, Eris, this is Captain Kukavi. That you, Marek?"*

"Pos, Dar, you dufftrooper. Redoubt's been placidated. I'm comming the code sequence that puts me in command of the fleet."

*"Shit,"* the voice of Kukavi said. *"Nothing personal, Marek, but Surdiakah hasn't devised a coherent attack plan for us, and you're hardly the sort of strategist to–"*

"Theba's left tit! Will you give me clearance to dock so I don't get fried by one of those myopic, hydrocephalic self-abusers you call DS gunners!"

*"You weren't given it by the comm-watch?"*

Eks took a slow, measured breath and released it slowly. "No," he said with sharp precision.

*"Well, come onboard already."*

*If I survive this,* Eks thought, *I'll send him on a Mind-running expedition to Shirash.*

*Eris/Verity* approached the Carnadyne Horde carefully, repulsor beams at full power. Maneuvering through the Carnadyne Void was hazardous at best, suicide at worst.

A volume of space dozens of light years in diameter, it contained no known stars (though any that might burn within the Void would be invisible to anyone more than half a light year away). It radiated infrared at 10 degrees Absolute, indicating that Something was going on in there. Whether it was the birthplace of new stars or a Sargasso of stellar detritus was uncertain. No one expressed any particular interest in studying the cloud of dust and rock. Not while astronomical behemoths such as the Maelstrom commanded attention.

It did make for a perfect hideout.

Eks cursed the choice. The dust, grasses, meteoroids, asteroids, and planetoids cluttering the Void made it anything but a void. Spacers had to travel at egregiously slow velocities. Too fast and the drifting garbage would pepper even the strongest cyprium hull protected by the most powerful meteor shields.

Too slow and one could spend a lifetime or twenty simply getting lost. The Carnadyne Void could as easily have been called the Okefenokee Swamp—or Baskerville Moor.

Marekallian prized *Eris* above anything short of his own life. Both were in danger in the Void. He practically crawled in his frantic haste to dock with the flagship.

After what seemed years of motion through the featureless realm, he caught sight of a flash of light from the fleet. A quick glance at the 'puter simulation indicated a distance of less than a hundred thousand kloms.

He squelched his first impulse, which was to shove the engines to full speed. Even though he could see the Horde, the space between them contained just as much matter as the previous megakloms. He had to take it just as slow. But *Eris* was only a few minutes away.

"Crew prepare to dock. Geb to the con. Ashtaru stand by DS. We are on constant battle alert. Klyjil—if either of them needs any assistance please give it. Ahamkara, you'll be coming with me onboard *Liberator*."

"No need to shout," her voice came from behind him. "I'm right here."

She stood in the hatchway bedecked in her finest (bedazzling) outfit. A flo-robe of indigo and lavender swirls draped from her (exposed) shoulders to her ankles. A sapphire-and-gold belt wrapped around her narrow waist and laced up, under, and between her breasts, accentuating their soft, jiggly fullness.

SpraYon gloves of pale blue reached up beyond her elbows. They ended at the same level as the top of her flo-robe, giving her a very broad-shouldered look that Eks would have found quite alluring under other circumstances. High heels of mauve strapwork and polychrome suspensors added to her height. She wore her TP camera unobtrusively in her hair, styled into a mass of intricate curls.

"Not exactly an outfit for a battle alert."

She smiled. "A former employer of mine taught me that appearance is everything."

"Former employer?"

"She disappeared." The banter seemed to trouble her.

"Then," Eks said, "appearance *isn't* everything. I've learned that *dis*appearance—at the right moment—can sometimes be everything, too."

"I'll keep that in mind."

*You're not disappearing as long I've left you unravished, Newser Tsadi. Phoenix isn't getting* all *the flash on this trip.*

The Carnadyne Horde grew and spread across their field of vision. Eks's pulse quickened in spite of his opinion of the fleet.

Geb entered quietly and took the first mate's chair. He watched Eks pilot the spacer. After a moment, he shifted his gaze to the much more interesting Ahamkara. Geb had little interest in spacecraft.

A single Orca could easily have stored fifty *Erises* within the confines of her hull with enough room left for them to rattle around loosely. Ahamkara watched as they passed one. She squinted to see the dark form of the Orca against the murky gray background. The spacer grew. And grew. It filled the viewing port until she felt as if she were falling endlessly toward it.

The dreadnought's surface bristled with weaponry. She had no idea of scale—plasma-pumped lasers as large as skyscrapers; pulsar beamers like ancient Homeworld pyramids.

"See that hole in the prow? There's a particle beam accelerator running straight down the major axis for two kilometers. One pop from that and you could kiss a medium-sized city goodbye."

"Have they thought of, like, taking one to Bleak?"

Eks smiled. "A little humor, finally?"

"No, just bringing it down to your level."

Eks frowned, tapping a few course corrections into SIPACUM. *Maybe I'll drug her, first.*

*Verity/Eris* maneuvered past the first dreadnought, around a small knot of support spacers clustered around a fuel pod and inward toward another Orca.

All about them, ships filled the darkness. The dust in the Void was not thick enough at this distance to provide aerial perspective. Every ship stood out in sharp relief wherever the beam of a worklight or warning beacon flashed. No sun provided light to illuminate the Horde.

Relying mostly on SIPACUM's ranging, the Mindrunner hard-docked his spacer with *Liberator*. He let out a long sigh and powered the ship down.

"Geb," he said. "When Ahamkara and I board *Liberator*, unzip *Verity* and pull her a few thousand kloms from the perimeter of the fleet. Firm?"

"Firm."

Eks offered his arm to Tsadi, tilting his head and saying, "May I escort you onboard the flagship of our rag-tag fleet?"

Through her gracious smile, she said, "I hope you know I'm not the sort to be swaved by courtliness."

*Nor the sort to employ any sort of diplomacy,* he mused, but smiled right back at her.

Onboard *Liberator,* Eks and Tsadi were passed quickly through security by a young Jarp who lacked a translahelm. The spacer's powerful engines, even though operating only to keep the ship powered up on standby and to maintain its slow rotation for "gravity," sent an odd vibration through the plasteel deckplates.

The newser felt an unease envelop her as they were taken to Captain Kukavi.

He was a man of moderate height, Ahamkara noted; 175 sems max. He wore a tight-fitting crimson tunic with terracotta skinTites from the waist down. His boots were of the light, EZ-walk fighter design. His most striking features were those above his thin, rugged face.

Captain Kuvaki was as bald as a polykel ball bearing. His scalp, though, bore an astonishingly intricate pattern of scarlet, orange, and rust-hued tattoos. On the left side of his head, from eyebrow to ear, a poorly healed (and, amazingly, never cytologically repaired) scar formed a low ridge that arced across the tattoo like a knife-slash through a painting.

His voice was as disturbingly intense as the throb of *Liberator*'s engines.

"We've replayed the copy *C!* message you commed us. The carrier beam also contained a coded message giving us Redoubt's location so that we can send a rescue ship. I've dispatched *Spirit of Graha.*"

"That leaves us with forty-two Orcas, pos?" Eks's gaze roamed over the telits in the large command center.

A dozen men and women, four Jarps, and a Crozer monitored the computer-guided activities of the Horde.

"How about TGW deployment?" The Mindrunner was trying to grill the captain without sounding hurried, and it was a definite effort.

"No unusual movements," Kukavi said. "And please tell your *friend* there to shut off her camera."

Ahamkara almost sneered.

Eks turned on her. "This is off the record, got it? This is *not* part of the Kabeshunt story."

"News," Ahamkara Tsadi said with the serene arrogance of her insensitive kind, "is news."

"You b—"

Marekallian broke that off and took her firmly by the arm. He pulled her aside—an easy feat in the ship's .4G. Her eyes went wide, then narrowed and her mouth firmed. He ignored that, and spoke low and intensely.

"Listen, sweetheart. I'm all for publicity and openness— I invited you, remember? We are, unfortunately, onboard a battle spacer that may be under attack at any moment. Kindly grant the captain of the ship his prerogatives. He's the sort of man who spaces people who disagree with him. Can't you see that in those eyes of his? Where do you think he got those tattoos—watching Akima Mars?"

Tsadi stiffened. Her narrowed eyes had widened again and now she blinked twice. She switched off her TP.

Marekallian's hand left her arm as if it had never been there. "Captain Kukavi," he said, walking over to the viewing port. Outside, spacecraft seemed to fill the universe. "I am going to disperse the fleet."

Bodies reacted while all ears in the command center turned their attention to him.

*"What?!"* Kukavi stared as if one glance could sear Eks into nothingness.

Marekallian let them all see his sigh. "We can't defeat the combined forced of TGO and TGW by sheer firepower," he told the captain, aware of others listening. "The attack on Redoubt is proof enough that the arm of TGO has already stretched out to put its fingers into our most secret enclave."

He turned to address the others oncon. "A pair of Orcas will be assigned to every Protected planet on the charts. They and certain support craft will engage in accelerated Mindrunning activities on those planets. The goal of educating whole planets to reject their oppressors will be a far simpler and safer task than open attack on TGW bases."

He paused for dramatic effect, and continued just as Kukavi opened his mouth.

"The Orcas will also serve to defend the people of the planets from slavers and looters—" (his voice caught for just an instant on the word)—"and any others who violate their sovereignty."

*Marek's losing it again,* Kukavi mused.

"We're to gain our allies from those who have the most to gain from joining us," Eks said, making it a ringing declaration, "—the primitives to whom we'll bring the benefits of civilization and the freedom of the spaceways!"

No one applauded. Everyone merely stared, the Crozer with all three eyes. Eks saw frowns here and there.

"I'm afraid, *Myrzha* Eks," the captain said, "that since the Council of Ninety-Three was not completely eliminated, there are still some strategists who might like to exercise their privileges?" He ended the statement as if it were a tactful question.

Eks bitterly flipped his fingers downward. "We don't have time to drag some theorizing fradgitator over here, *Captain*. We are in the midst—"

They were. The intruder alert cut off all debate.

# 16

There is a violence that liberates, and a violence that enslaves; there is a violence that is moral and a violence that is immoral.

—Benito Mussolini

"I told you—I just inslotted the cassette and we took off!" Trafalgar Cuw did his best to look repentent.

Sweetface wasn't buying it. "From the moment we started searching for Janja, things have been happening too coincidentally. I know I'm not a member of the Coalition, but I *am* a member of the crew. And I don't like this situation one byte."

"Sweetface is right, Traf." Cinnabar looked at the other four assembled in the con-cabin.

Quindy kept her gaze on the telits, stealing occasional glances at her crew. Cinnabar sat in the first mate's chair. Kalahari, dressed in her gray exercise outfit, leaned against the far bulkhead and sulked. She tugged at strands of her newly platinum hair, watching the exchange.

Sweetface paced around the cabin, watching the Outie. "We all know he has some sort of fake TGO Prime ID. Or is it? He says he's been following his 'hunches.' Where does he get them? And now this. He inslots a cassette and we nearly get torn apart hottailing it straight into the Void!" It paused and looked at Quindy.

"Trafalgar? Where did you find it?" she asked, without turning to face her lover.

Trafalgar hesitated. The others weren't sure whether it was part of his act or not.

"I was testing the system to see—"

"I'd already run five checks. You knew that. Please don't give me scut, Traf."

"I won't be able to convince you of anything if you don't—"

"*Black Dawn*'s setting out after us. I guess she didn't like the way we left without saying goodbye." Cinnabar squirmed in its seat to avoid the sore spots on its buttocks. "That Tura's one rough . . . person."

Kalahari snorted.

"None of this really matters." Quindy's smoky eyes glanced at a blood-red telit. "SIPACUM's been taken over. Removing the cassette hasn't interrupted the program." She looked at Cuw with smoldering resentment. "I am captain of this ship, and Janja is the owner. Our lives and her ship are in danger at this velocity, Traf."

"Well," he drawled, "of course I'm no expert, but I suspect that we're moving at just about the upper limit of safety. Maybe the program bug will work itself out in a while."

"Is that another *hunch?*" Sweetface stared its unspoken accusation.

SIPACUM buzzed for attention. Quindy swung around and read her screen.

"Something's dead ahead. Big asteroids or—"

The engines cut off.

"See?" Cuw grinned. "I told you it would shape up. I'm *not* an expert mechanic, but dammit, I do good work. It's *fixed.*"

"Some fix. We're drifting toward enough spacers to choke the Maelstrom."

"What!" The rest of the crew stared at Quindy. Trafalgar's smile was imperceptible.

*"Attention intruder!"* a voice snapped over the comm.

"I think that sets the tone for the rest of the conversation," Kalahari muttered on her way out of the cabin.

*"You are outnumbered and out-powered. You will be taken in tow. Do not attempt to resist. We do not want your ship, your cargo, or you. Confirm."*

Quindy stared with imploring eyes at Trafalgar.

His face revealed nothing. His mind raced. *All right, Captain Quindy. You've done exceptionally well up to now. Keep going. I'll catch you if you fall.*

She turned back to the comm-mike. "This is Captain Quindarissa Gh778328s of spacer *Sunmother*. We—" She looked again at Cuw, then back to the mike. "We are complying with your *request*."

She switched off the comm and avoided the gaze of the rest of the crew.

"Set your stoppers on Two and be calm."

She hoped that Trafalgar Cuw had not betrayed her...

Tura ak Saiping was lying on the elaborate couch in her dungeon when the alarm sounded.

She wore a black equhyde strap-titser, thigh-length ebony bucket-boots, black leather gloves, and not much else besides sweat. Satiated by her trysts with Kalahari and with Cinnabar, she floated in a hot, drifting realm of memory.

*No one leaves TGO.* She hadn't understood what that meant until Randy died. *It must have been Sinchung Sin,* she mused for the thousandth time. *He will Die.*

And her loins warmed again.

She rubbed the handle of the whip against her clitoris, prepared to thrust it again into herself. Equhyde boots squeaked against the equhyde couch to which she had strapped her body.

The alarm startled her, but did not unsettle her. Jumping off the couch, she kicked toward the hatch. In a few seconds she reached the con and discovered the nature of the alert.

*Sunmother* was blasting away from *Black Dawn* on a trajectory that took it through Roche's Alley straight into the Carnadyne Void.

*Flainers!* She threw a set of switches and punched the drive into life. *If they're off to tell tales on this little pirate, they're in for a fight!*

The acceleration shoved her back in her chair. Her full round breasts flattened almost to saucers and her mouth stretched.

*Black Dawn*'s engines were more than equal to overtaking *Sunmother*. The head start had to be overcome, though, and that took some time. Time enough for *Sunmother* to reach the Carnadyne Horde.

Tura's more sensitive equipment detected the fleet before the other spacer had, even though she was far behind. She instantly reversed thrust and decelerated. Satisfied that she had matched velocity with that of the mysterious cluster of spacecraft, she cut all power to the ship and monitored the capture of *Sunmother* on passive sensors.

Her right hand never strayed from its position above the DS button.

Marekallian Eks surveyed the boarding of the prisoners. A woman who looked twenty-five but was probably sixty or so stood beside him. Her hair hung past her shoulders in a not displeasing display of kinks and waves.

Ahamkara stood on his other side, recording and staring with fascination. "It's, like, totally *tense* onboard," she whispered into her lapel mike.

"The ship is a modified yacht," the other woman said to Eks. "It can't be an accident that they found us. Captain Kukavi will want them all questioned."

Eks nodded, watching the crew of the captured spacer as they came through the umbilical one at a time.

The first was a woman, whose black skin faintly glistened. She was blacker than most Galactics. Eks figured the skin tone to be a celldye job. Her bright jonquil hair could be nothing else. A bright red one-piece suit sheathed her lovely body and a black sash circled her waist. The long, swinging ends of the sash were cut on the bias. She carried herself with pride and dignity.

Eks felt immediate response to her sensuous call, and tried to put it out of his mind.

The second woman was as skinny as the first was rounded. Her hair was short and platinum-dyed. She wore an identical black-sashed red jumpsuit. The sneer on her face was prideful, but hardly dignified.

*Intriguing. Maybe they're a pair.*

Two Jarps followed the two women. One was dressed in the same sort of scarlet uniform. The other sported a tight blue halter top and matching shorts. It had a translahelm. The one in red didn't.

*They might serve as possible allies. Jarps have no love for the established order.* "Is that it?" he asked of the woman at his side.

"I think there's one m—"

*"And get your stinking hands off me!"* The voice resounded through the umbilical and into the staging area.

*No—It can't be!* Eks stepped forward to see the man who strode onboard *Liberator* as if he owned it. At sight of him, the Mindrunner's eyes rivaled Klyjil's in diameter.

He was garbed in the red jumpsuit of the majority, topping it off with an eleven-gallon Wayne and bottoming out with garish royal blue boots. His dark eyes scanned the hold. A guard struggled in his grasp, trying to release the man's hand from the nape of his neck.

"Somebody put this grat on a leash." He tossed the guard forward. The other guards instantly surrounded him, stoppers drawn. His hands raised in placation. "Hey, sadiki. Don't get fradgitated. I'm friendly when petted."

"Trafalgar Cuw, you flaining son of a *bitch!*"

The crew of *Sunmother* stared at the angry man in khaki. Trafalgar grinned weakly.

"Why, uh—Marekallian, old jacko! What sort of scam are you running out here? I mean—pleased to meet you."

Eks made a violent motion with one hand. "Forget it, Cuw. I'm not cutting you in on this one. Forget you saw any of this. Just as *I* had to forget the Eyes of Kilre!"

Trafalgar flipped five. "Marek, Marek! That was *years* ago. I lost them in a velletrom game the next week. You never could take a gag, could you?"

Eks stared in silent fury at the other Outreacher. When he spoke, he calculated every word to sting.

"Your darling cousin Calcutta couldn't take a joke either, could she?"

Cuw's smile remained plastered on, though Quindy thought it now seemed artificial, strained. *What sort of volcano is brewing beneath that cool landscape?* she wondered, and suddenly felt a twinge of sorrow for the mysterious man who shared his bed with her but never his secrets.

The lack of reaction disturbed Marekallian. He turned to the woman on his left.

"I'll take personal custody of these people. Thank you. Stow their weapons onboard their spacer and post a guard." He looked the crew over once again. "Make that four guards."


"If you were around Jonuta," Janja said, "you know how I came to the spaceways."

HReenee sat next to her in the con-cabin. The computer

scanned the Void for neutrino flux. Janja watched the computer screen. HReenee watched Janja.

And she remembered Jonuta. What she felt for the daring, roguishly handsome slaver was something beyond fondness; something approaching love. It was more than infatuation— she considered both her and her feelings more mature than that word implied.

"He kidnapped me, HReenee. Killed my intended mate, my lover. Sold me as a slave. I was brutalized, beaten. But never broken."

"He's dead now," HReenee said.

"I know, HReenee."

"News travels fa—"

"I killed him."

HReenee moaned weakly and lowered her head. "Then I must kill you? You have killed my lover and kidnapped me."

"I killed an evil man, HReenee. And you came here of your own will."

Yellow eyes regarded eyes of storm gray. "You tricked me."

The HRal said nothing for awhile, then made an elegant gesture with her claws extended. First the left one withdrew into her middle finger, followed by the one on her right.

"We must have a truce," she told the Aglayan. "I desire very much to be a part of TGO."

*I'll just bet you do,* Janja thought. *That would serve your secret purpose quite nicely, wouldn't it?* She chose her words carefully.

"As an agent, a HRal would hardly be inconspicuous."

"Neither is an Aglayan."

"At least I look human."

Janja recognized her error the moment it left her lips. She realized that she should have said, "I *am* human." The more-than-human chewed at her lip, hoping that the slip would pass unnoticed.

She had to admit, though, that the HRal would make a superb agent. The skill of a predator and the silence of a cat!

Half a ship away from the con, Ratran Yao confronted the Iceworld Connection, the...*being* called Carnadyne. He lay on his cabin's bed, adjusting the gain on his mind-comm headset.

"Come on, Carnadyne," he thought. "Where in Musla's cold hell are you?"

*"Right where I usually am, Cougar—in my laboratory."*

He breathed an agitated sigh. "Where is that fleet of ships you detected in the Void?"

*"Why are you bothering with that?"* Her telepathic voice was unemotionally quizzical. *"You know what a fleet of dreadnoughts can do."*

"Yes. Which is why I–"

*"Aren't you more interested in what's happening on Shir-ash?"*

"No, dammit. I'm–" Her statement sank in. *"What* is happening on Shirash?"

*"A spacer splashed down with a crew of five plus eighteen passengers. They're still alive."*

*Galactics?* he thought with alarm. *In the telehypnotic grasp of those jellyblobs?*

*"Yes. And the spacer is probably still functional."*

"Stop that!"

*"Stop what, Cougar?"* Carnadyne asked, mystified.

"Reading my mind!"

*"How can I avoid it when you're wearing my mind-comm?"*

"Carnadyne—please. Just give me the coordinates of the fleet!"

She did, and he tore the strapwork helmet from his head.

*Shirash! Dammit, Rantanagar, why'd you have to try to leave TGO when there's so much to* do? *I could use you now.*

Ratran Yao quietly fed the coordinates into SIPACUM.

# 17

... the least objectionable form of armed force is that which springs up voluntarily ... and disbands as soon as the occasion which called it into existence is past: that the really desirable thing is that all men ... should be at peace; and to reach this, all peaceful persons should withdraw their support from the army and require that all who make war shall do so at their own cost and risk; that neither pay nor pensions are to be provided for those who choose to make man-killing a trade.

—Voltairine De Cleyre

Marekallian Eks never let his attention wander from the varicolored telits of his spacer's console for more than a few seconds. He oversaw the Horde's movements and spoke to his ... guest with a comfortably divided concentration.

Trafalgar Cuw sat in the chair next to Eks, his dazzlingly brilliant boots up on a console, ankles crossed, arms behind his neck. A long lean line of red in the Coalition jumpsuit, he stared at the dark images beyond the viewport.

"Since I'm going to kill all of you anyway," Eks said, "I might as well tell you all of my plans in minute detail." He smiled briefly at the other Outie, and turned his gaze back to the console.

*That's what the villain always does,* Trafalgar thought; *it's tradition. My job is to try to avoid the dying part, dear ole buddy.* He said:

"I'm waiting, Marek."

"Ah, Traf, my old drinking jacko. You don't think I was engineered to be stupid, do you?"

Trafalgar's voice was lazily equable: "You're here, aren't you?"

"What's stupid about fighting for freedom? I come from a grand tradition."

"You *claim* a grand tradition, Marek. So do all other would-be tyrants."

"Tyrant!" Eks shifted his gaze to Trafalgar for a long moment. He looked genuinely hurt. "Would a tyrant have dispersed the Horde into Mindrunning instead of attacking TGO?" He sighed. "Remember back on Outreach? I'd just arrived from Resh, hot and reckless. Got my new name, ready for a new start. No more being a priest's son. I ran into you in that bar—hey, I never did thank you for dropping that narcobum. Too drunk. Say—why *did* you save my neck, then?"

Trafalgar snorted. "Just a stupid mistake. He only had thirty sems and about fifty kilos on you. Should've let him vivisect you."

Eks looked almost ready to smile. He didn't. "Spacer *Kimben*," he said into the comm-mike. "You and *Sabbah* depart for Aglaya. Contact Dispatch for the support spacers that will accompany you. Be careful, now—they're scrappy iron-age 'barbarians.' Your navigator—N'Mboodra?—she's familiar with their culture. Let her make first contact."

*"Firm."* The terse reply was both forced and restrained.

Marekallian swung back to Trafalgar. "What a team we were, Traf! All clear and on green, Cuw-Eks, Cuw-Eks. Remember that?"

Trafalgar winced. "I'd prefer to forget it."

"And those garish Outie-fits. As you see, I've toned it down. Doesn't pay to startle the natives."

"Marek—" Looking boyishly open, Trafalgar assumed

his best soft-soap tones. "Can't you see that this is all a ridiculous folly? Doomed from the start?"

"Oh, the Horde had its problems." (Eks was watching the computer simulations of the ships' movements with narrowed eyes.) "But I think I've straightened them out. Direct attacks on TGW would be suicidal. This is much more preferable."

"Oh, undoubtedly." Trafalgar Cuw uncrossed his ankles and dropped his feet from the console. He leaned forward conspiratorially, tipping back his Wayne and lowering his voice. "But TGO wouldn't even deign to notice the actions of your Council if you'd just kept a low profile and two sets of records."

"The Council was more than just an organization of counter-economists, Traf! They were dedicated to freeing the Galaxy!"

Trafalgar nodded. "Uh-huh. Sure, Marek, sure. I know that." *My ass. Just as you were dedicated to "freeing 'oppressed' people of Protected planets"—so long as you get to loot their archival and religious treasure-houses, dear moralistic old friend.* "Do you, uh, maybe think, though, that they could have won that glowing battle by economic means? A little *baksheesh* in the right places can work wonders."

The Mindrunner jerked his head around. "Don't you think I tried to convince them of that? They'd had it with bribes. Individually and as the Council, they'd bought off quite a number of policers including some TAI people. And you'd be surprised how many TGW superspooks look the other way, for a price. Then the Council discovered a force that couldn't be bribed. Flain it, it can't even be *found!* The Gray Organization."

"So—can't find 'em to bribe, stomp 'em out, hmm? So they—you—resort to war."

Eks started. "War? This isn't war. This is revolt."

Trafalgar wiggled a finger. "That's not a finger, it's a digit." He shrugged. "Call it what you want. Those dreadnoughts have one purpose, and that's destruction. That's war, Marek—assuming that someone fights back, of course. If no one does, then it's massacre. War, murder, massacre, revolt. War, no matter what you name it. And that is sure to attract TGO's attention."

"Pursuit of freedom is not an act of war. You—more than anyone, Traf, you—ought to know that." He glanced back at the screen. "Scramble, out there," he shouted into the mike. "You redshift in fifteen mins. What are you, chulwars?"

His index finger began tapping impatiently on the chair arm. He glanced at Trafalgar, looked at the screen as he spoke.

"I brought you up here with the hope that you'd see my reasoning and join me. What I'm doing will free the Galaxy, Traf. Maybe not for all time, maybe not everywhere. It's *education,* Trafalgar. Brainboosts, medicine, trade, a raising of consciousness and cultures. On the level, Traf. You know it's what I've always sought—ever since I saw what I saw on Resh. Slavery is *ugly,* Trafalgar Cuw! And TGO won't stop it. Yet TGO tries to stop *me.* What does that make them, old friend?"

Trafalgar shook his head. Pulling off his Wayne, he tapped a few specks of dust from the broad brim and settled it back onto his head. *It's like lecturing a petulant child, damn it. Trouble is, the child's both intelligent and now, dangerous!*

"War, jacko," he said. "TGO doesn't strike unless it perceives a threat of *war.* You know why TGO exists—to prevent *war.* It doesn't chase slavers unless they get together a nasty-looking fleet—or really challenges TGO, and hurts—and it doesn't trouble itself with Mindrunners either . . . unless they get together a nasty-looking fleet." He glanced meaningfully at the console's screen. "TGO exists only to prevent war. It's done resoundingly well, you know?"

"And it's a monolith that perceives any resistance to *it* as a threat of war!" Eks said, with a mixture of petulance and accusation.

He made an angry gesture and looked at the screen for a quiet moment. When he turned his attention back to the fellow Outreacher with whom he had only that planetary origin in common, the pitch of his voice had risen half an octave.

"It's the first sign of arrogant tyranny! It always has been. Now TGO drains our wealth by forcing planets to pay for 'protection,' yet we're ever the prey of pirates, slavers, and murderers."

"And graverobbers."

Eks didn't even hear the cut. In a fanatic's soliloquy, he was nearly oblivious to the other man and to the movement and multicolored flashing of computer simulations and tel-its.

"A despot can rule a planet with a bloody fist and TAI won't even pay a visit, but—"

(*Not true,* Trafalgar Cuw thought, but saw no reason to interrupt a man whose mouth was made up.)

"—but the instant the ruler raises its gaze from one planet and seeks to challenge TGO's dominance of the spaceways, The Gray Organization unleashes its wrath!"

(*That is, it does the job it's paid for,* Trafalgar thought, shifting his buttocks for a more comfortable attendance of the lecture.)

"The *peasants* are Kept In Line," Marekallian Eks said, and seemed to have come to a pause.

Trafalgar flipped his fingers. "You've always had a sore spot where TGO was concerned, Marek. Did it have anything to do with why you and your brother *had* to leave Resh and come to Outreach? Why you and Denverdarian felt compelled to change your names?"

"Denvo is dead, Traf. I rather suspect it was at the hands of TGO."

"That's nothing new. You *always* suspect TGO." *And I guess it's about time I did something brave and brilliant. Wish I could think of something not guaranteed to get me killed.*

"And I'm always ri–*what is it?*"

An alarm wailed into nerve-jangling activity.

"Intruder alert!" a woman snapped, two stations down.

Marekallian frowned. "Intercept immediately." He turned a glowering look on Trafalgar Cuw. "Friends of yours?"

"I didn't leave a forwarding address, as I recall."

Eks turned jerkily back to the woman. "Well, have them– Oh!"

He jerked as if struck; Trafalgar Cuw grunted, squinted, and averted his face as the ships at the outer perimeter exploded into blinding light.

Thousand of kloms from the fleet, Tura ak Saiping floated lightly against the chair's straps. She watched the destruction of the spacers of the Horde in total silence. Her breath quickened at sight of the sun-white flashes. Like new stars being born, they lit up the scene of destruction for her own vision and that of her passive receptors. The computer simulation onscreen was the only powered equipment she allowed just now.

What she saw quickened her pulse and accelerated her breath.

She was very glad that she was where she was.

Ratran Yao coordinated the other two killer ships with Janja's. Janja watched the inhumanly fast Defense Systemry and acted as a (more than) human override.

"Sweep across," Yao said into the comm-mike. "Have DS synchronize missiles so that they hit the next flank simultaneously."

"Majority of ships' DS actuated," the computer said in a voice faster than a human's could form the words, yet just as understandable.

"Second salvo—*launch!*" Janja snapped.

She watched the scores of missiles blast away from the weapons clusters like the seeds of some murderous version of a Jahpurese dandelion. Seconds later, the viewport automatically darkened to protect their eyes from the actinic flashes of matter and anti-matter colliding in mutual annihilation.

Janja had no time to think of individuals, of crew, of killing. She was destroying ships. She simply pushed buttons, and killed. Quickly. Efficiently. As cold, unfeeling and indiscriminate as the hardrain of Aglaya.

"I don't know, damn it!" Geb furiously actuated *Eris*'s DS, powered up every protective screen he could remember, and tried to make the ship as invisible as possible. "I can't tell whether *Liberator*'s been hit—it's like a lightning storm out there!"

Ashtaru strapped into the DS chair. Her electric blue hair-spikes hung in limp, sweaty tangles. She stared at the battle monitor with grim fatalism, her teeth gritting nervously together. She saw no battle; she was looking at annihilation.

Klyjil/Phoenix stood behind her, silently watching the systematic destruction of the Carnadyne Horde. He felt a terrible fear seeking to whelm and consume him. *If this is what they are, these "humans," then they are like mad children* given a god's power. His fear was replaced by an overwhelming sadness.

Klyjil bazRakava wept for this strange race. And for the Akil.

"DS up!" Marekallian Eks cried. "Full shields!"

"Already initiated," the DSer reported.

"Meteor shields at full intensity!"

"Firm."

Actuating the *defense* portion of "Defense" Systemry (and being at the center of the Horde) saved *Liberator* from immediate destruction. Other Orcas, reacting too slowly or powering up the offensive portion of DS, were caught off guard. The nearly invisible spacegoing missiles hit with the force of small nuclear bombs. Impact meant detonation; detonation meant incandescence; incandescence meant instant painless annihilation.

The gray of the Carnadyne Void was turned to the coruscant white of a Syrian B-type star. The wan cold light of distant stars vanished completely, occulted by the greater, awful brightness around *Liberator*. Shrapnel and slag from destroyed spacecraft bounced off the flagship's shields. It lay rocking in the center of a sphere of blinding immolation.

*The Big Bang*, Trafalgar Cuw thought, and reacted as swiftly as Eks.

Grabbing the comm-mike, he punched up a full-spectrum broadcast.

"Attention! Attention!" he shouted, as if sheer volume could drive his words through the explosion-rocked vacuum. "Input follows: Tee Gee Oh one two three three three R-Revolt three eight eight six R-Retreat P-Protest A-Attack. Got that? T, G, O, 1,2,3,3,3, R-3, 8, 8, 6, R-P-A!"

The message reached the killer ships. Ratran Yao heard it and blinked, then frowned. "Get that?"

"Firm," the computer said. "Input. Processing."

Janja's breath caught. *That's Trafalgar! Trafalger is onboard that ship!* Her hands froze their grip on arms of the ship-chair . . .

... While on *Liberator*, Marekallian Eks dealt with the message in his own way. He pounced for Trafalgar Cuw's throat.

"You flaining bastard slipsucking *traitor!*" His fingers tightened around the other man's trachia with a madman's strength.

Trafalgar struggled under the assault, his face swiftly purpling. One bright-booted foot whipped up and shoved at Marek's stomach. They tumbled out of the chair and rolled to the deckplates.

Trafalgar forced fingers under Eks's grasp enough to let him choke out words: "It's—only—chance! Fleet's dead. I mi—ight be—uh!—able to save—usss."

"Betray me, you mean! You sisterslicin' sellout!"

"I—never—bought—*in!*"

*This damned scuzgrat's Strong*, Trafalgar thought, rolling his eyes in search of leverage, weapon, or help. He saw only that everyone else oncon was too concerned with trying to save *Liberator* to worry about the battling Outies. Besides, their hero Marek Eks had the situation well in hand, the situation being Trafalgar's throat. *Why do I do these dam' heroic things?!*

Captain Kukavi was sweatily working to find a way out of the carnage without taking the desperate last resort of jam-cramming. *Wish they'd kill each other*, the beleaguered captain thought, and that was the only attention he gave the two very, very troublesome Outreachers. Three Orcas and dozens of support ships had already jam-crammed; gone City. Where or whether they would reappear was unknown. Kukavi had no desire to join them.

Quindy headed for the con at the first sound of the alarm. She entered to see Eks busily strangling Trafalgar while everyone else minded its own business—and the ship's.

"Traf—wha—" Quindy hesitated only an instant to appraise the situation, which was that Trafalgar Cuw's face was about two shades darker, definitely showing purple, and his tongue was protruding. "Oh shit."

With a mighty swing of one red-sheathed leg, Quindy kicked Marekellian Eks in the balls.

He reacted in the standardly accepted manner.

Sucking in a noisily wheezy breath, he spasmodically jerked into a fetal position. His fingers clenched once against Cuw's throat, flexed open, retracted, and relocated themselves in the general area of his groin.

Trafalgar rolled free and stood. His hands replaced Eks's at his own throat, a lot more tenderly. He staggered as if he'd just spent six hours in a drinking contest, and looked worse than that.

"Didn't anyone ever teach you not to discuss politics at social gatherings, Traf m'love?" Quindy grinned and handed him a stopper. It felt nice in his hand, warm from hers. Comforting. "I got that off a guard who fainted when the action started," she said. "Shall we stroll?"

Trafalgar stared down at the contorted, vomiting figure on the deck.

"I suppose. Our host seems to have no objections." He squatted to relieve Eks of his stopper, which he passed to Quindy. "Ah, now you look better! Where're the others?"

"On their way now."

Trafalgar Cuw smiled. "Then let's blow this joint."

No one bothered to have a go at stopping them. All eyes glazed with panic and terror at the devastation their screens displayed. They tried to save themselves and the others around them from an enemy they could not even locate. The two red-jumpsuited individuals departed their company.

Quindy and Trafalgar ran through the ship's tunnels like crimson flames. Dazed, panicky crewmembers rushed about in a common frenzy fed by each other. They clogged access hatches to escape pods and struggled with emergency pressure suits. A few loud voices tried to restore order. Some responded. Most didn't. Someone punched the owner of a loud voice.

Quindy stoppered seven people clustered around the umbilical to *Sunmother*'s locked hatch. She used the number Two setting. Instead of dancing, the would-be escapers dropped as if they'd had their plugs pulled.

"Ah—the nice man carried a modified stopper. Fun!"

"Did you know they're being made illegal on various planets and stations," Trafalgar gasped, as they hopped over strewn bodies, all quite alive and quite unconscious.

"Figures," Quindy said, and raced up the gentle ramping curve of the umbilical with her companion close behind.

At the locked hatch, he whirled and dropped to one knee, covering their wake with leveled stopper. He heard her shout "Yaood Pilishishi!" and before he could wonder what the vug their Ghanji gem-dealer friend had to do with anything, he found out. The name was the code to unseal the airlock.

"Cute," he muttered, backing after her. "No one else's likely to try *that* as an Open Cess-me." Then he was up and leaping into the ship after good old Quindy.

"Zip us up and redshift," she shouted, hardly noticing that she was issuing commands as effortlessly and assuredly as the best of captains.

Trafalgar noticed. Even in their precipitate haste, he had time to feel proud of the achievement. He also scrambled to the con ahead of her and seized the commsender.

"Attention attacking spacers. If you're reading what I think you're reading, you know enough to let this ship go. Sure would appreciate it." He nodded to Quindy and Cinnabar, and switched off the comm for an instant. "Inslot the jam-cram cassette. Punch it if I say 'apple'. Uh, please, Captain!"

Cinnabar inslotted the cassette and waited. The CAGS-VIC input the command word and confirmed it vocally.

"Now we sit tight and sweat them out."

"What," Quindy asked without interrupting her super-vision of the ship's power-up cycle, "if whoever's attacking us doesn't *like* TGO Agents Prime?"

"Or someone imitating one," he smiled, to let her know he recognized a trap even under such pressure. "Then we go Forty Percent City. Or they kill us."

He tried to force a Shaitan-may-care smile, and couldn't.

# 18

Putting the pacifism principle in one's mind seems to have
the effect of ingesting a psychoactive drug. Flashes of brilliant insight and otherwise inconceivable innovation result,
but mostly what comes out is a distorted view of reality.
                                        —Samuel Edward Konkin III


Ratran Yao gazed at the readout, mystified. The letters stood
out in eye-eez turquoise against the flat black background.

*What in Booda's backyard is an Agent Prime doing on-
board a spacer slated for TGO placidation? Is this some
sly trick? Who could be that much in the know without being
part of us?*

He left the flagship alone for a moment and checked the
battle report. Thirty-eight Orca-class craft destroyed or dis-
abled. Three jam-crammed. That left the dreadnought at the
center. One hundred-seven support ships dead or crippled
by proximity to the anti-matter explosions and the resulting
flak.

He debated using the weapon Carnadyne had off-
handedly developed for him. The dreadnought was secure
against the missiles now. Its powerful shields were more
than a match for anything other than another dreadnought's
DS.

Except for one item in the arsenal. A particle-beam pulsar
utilizing highly energized *anti*-particles. He held off for a

moment. *One of my Primes, hmm? And why the flaining hell don't I know about it?*

"Redshift, Two and Three. We'll handle the cleanup from this end."

Janja listened to another comm-band. The confused, frantic transmissions from spacer to spacer overlapped, interfered, interwove into a unified jumble of grief, fear, and pain.

*They're dying just the same as their enemies would have done. Alone, terrified, helpless. Thingmakers discovering in the final moments of their lives that nothing can save them. No thing will ever save them.*

## MEANWHILE

"Give it just enough thrust to make it look as if we're breaking away by accident," Quindy said, and watched Trafalgar silently program SIPACUM with the order. The command was too semantically loaded to try to explain to the VIC.

The ship lurched once and drifted free. The short-lived hiss of atmosphere escaping from the ruptured umbilical conducted through the hull into the con-cabin. *Sunmother* crawled away from *Liberator* into the morass of waste that had been the Carnadyne Horde.

"Easy," Trafalgar muttered to no one in particular. "Easy on the way out and maybe we'll get clear. No word from the attackers?"

"They could be long gone for all they seem to be doing."

"I could live with that," Cinnabar said fervently.

Trafalgar slid a cassette into the active slot, next to the jam-cram cassette. "Here's where we make our getaway, my dears . . . Theba willing." *Right, Theba baby? You don't want such a deceitful rascal as I am in the Otherworld, do you?* "Initiate!"

The cassette ordered SIPACUM to find a SafePoint for Tachyon Conversion/SPTC, and to take the spacer and its edgy occupants into "subspace" to defeat infinity—with only a single buzz as fifteen seconds warning. How long it would take to find a safe point in the midst of the Void was anybody's guess.

Trafalgar determined not to waste the time. He moved closer to Quindy and grasped her waist with strong, loving arms.

"It's a race between mathematics and psychology now, Captain Quindaridi." A firm squeeze accompanied his utterance of her Ghanjese name—the name under which she had once been disgraced.

She didn't flinch. Her hand reached up to touch his, to stroke it lovingly.

She looked up at him, bright yellow tresses framing her obsidian face. "I love you, *Myrzha* Cuw."

He smiled back. His lips sought hers. Their tongues caressingly explored familiar and ever-new regions.

Onboard *Liberator*, Marekallian Eks explored his own familiar regions. Gradually standing and trying to regain his lost breath, he surveyed the crew at their stations, oblivious to his pain. He ran a hand across his mouth to wipe the vomit from his face.

"Right," he said. He slowly unbent his body, twisting to see the Suzite newser recording his movements. Amusement was reflected in her thin smile.

Eris *moving in,* he noted. *Good. They wouldn't listen to me. To hell with them. To hell with the Council. From now on it's Eks for Eks, period.*

He took a deep breath. *Timing's everything. Get ready. One. Two.*

*Three!* He picked up the comm-mike and spoke in low tones.

"Geb. Dock at airlock seventeen and cycle your hatch. I'm going to jump."

"Firm," his first mate replied.

"Eks?" Ahamkara stepped toward the Mindrunner.

"One word and you get Fried." He pulled a ministopper from a jacket pouch. "I don't want anyone to notice I'm leaving. Stay put. Captain Kukavi likes newsers less than Geb does."

He backed toward the hatch.

Janja glanced nervously at Ratran, trying to *cherm* his disposition. She sensed only a mild bewilderment and an uncommon indecision.

"That small ship's getting away, Janja. Get it."

She zoomed in her TP view to see what she expected— the graceful lines of *Sunmother*. Her voice caught, her hand wavered. *Mother of Aglii, am I to kill my friends? No break with the past can be that complete. No loyalty can be that total. Help me, Sunmother!*

She watched the slow movement of the spacer bearing her god's name. Two of the missiles tracked it, ready to launch.

Yao noticed her hesitation. *All right, barbarian—you have a hunch and so have I. Let's play them both out.*

He switched on the comm. "Firm," he commed to the Orca and the smaller ship. "Readout is TGO Prime. On your way." He commed off. "Farkash—store that code for when we get back to base."

*I'll want to check on this Prime and see what I can find . . .*

Janja let go a tense breath. Rat watched her and nodded.

*Once again she's indebted to me. Fine. And so what if one dreadnought slips by? Poofing a Prime—if that's what he is—is a good deal more serious than doing in just any*

*TGO spear-bearer agent such as poor old Yanger. And Janje is very aware of having done that, in taking out Jonuta!*

Yao's mouth moved in a small, satirical smile. *Nice that he's still alive, ole Cap'm Cautious! A really clever one like that does wonders for R and D—and appropriations! We've already adopted . . . what?—two of his modifications and one brilliant trick! Thanks, Jonuta. I'll send 'er after you again some day. . . .*

"Take us home, Farkash," he said. He looked at Janja with his best sardonic imitation of a smile. "Good work, Janja. You still have to run into one of Ramesh Jageshwar's drones—and his sister's mighty testy in our durance vile!" *And I have to find out what the bloody hell's happening on Shirash.*

Then Ratran Yao, Janja and HReenee streaked away from the Carnadyne Horde-that-was at maximum velocity under Farkash's careful guidance.


"You're leaving without *Me?*" The shrill voice shattered the nervous concentration of *Liberator*'s con-watch and Captain Kukavi turned to stare at Ahamkara Tsadi—and Marekallian Eks.

"You cowardly traitor," he growled slowly. His stopper eased out of his holster and pointed at Eks.

"Brainless stash," Marekallian muttered, then turned to the captain and crew. "I'm sorry we can't part on more cordial footing. This is to announce my official resignation from the Council."

He stopper-beamed Kukavi.

The bald man danced to the tune of a number Two setting. The others oncon were torn between assisting their captain and continuing the life-or-death rescue operations controlled from their consoles.

They remained at their posts. Kukavi danced.

Eks placed a hand in the small of Tsadi's back and shoved with dignity-robbing force. She stumbled forward.

"So long, Ham." He flicked off the ministopper and redshifted into the tunnel.

The captain's helpless jiggle-shuffle ended as soon as Eks departed.

Ahamkara rose to her knees, then stood with a grunt. Kukavi looked at her and shook his head. He turned to speak calmly into the intraship comm.

"General Alert. This is the Captain. If any of you happens to see Marekallian Eks—khaki clothes, black hair queued in black—*Fry* him. Unless you have something important to attend to. Captain out."

He turned to see Newser Tsadi racing away from the con. Captain Kukavi sighed, shrugged, turned away. *Liberator* was a massive ship honeycombed with hundreds of kloms of passages, tunnels and tubeways. Eks knew where he was going. Ahamkara didn't. Captain Kukavi returned to business.

*Bastard knows where he's going and I don't,* Ahamkara Tsadi thought—and followed the trail of fallen or dazed crew that Eks left in his wake.

She caught sight of him on a straightaway and fought not to lose his khaki'd back. She hardly paused to squat and pick up a stopper from a man in orange coveralls. She used it. Fortunately it was set on number One, since she had about as much knowledge of stoppers as she did of spaceship drives. Anyone who happened into her path froze in his tracks. Ahamkara found it a lot easier to run around and through crowds that way.

Her TP camera was recording it all.

*What a story, what a story,* she kept thinking. It ran through her mind like a poisoned mantra—along with another thought. *I'll kill you, Marek X! Nobody like abandons sweet little Kara!*

And, mouth firm, she ran. *Doing* something!

Her impatience, coupled with her lack of experience with stoppers, came close to undoing her. She beamed a woman with a One setting. Naturally the woman Froze and stayed right in Ahamkara's way.

"Out of the way, gratshit!" she snapped, and kicked viciously—at a woman already shivering under the paralysis beam.

The immediate result of the kick was that the stopper's effect was conducted into Ahamkara's body.

At that, she was lucky. Before it could affect her stride, her own momentum carried her on and that ghastly sensation ended. She continued, but rushed past others with rather more (enforced) courtesy.

Spotting Eks duck down a side tunnel, she skipped over a crewmember felled by him and followed the fleeing Outreacher. The distance she considered necessary to avoid his notice unfortunately also kept him beyond the reach of her stopper. She turned a corner and scrambled to a stop. Dead end!

She whipped about and headed the other way. The smell of ozone and grease marked the Mindrunner's path. She knew that odor from descriptions on the holo. *Marek's Fried someone. Or gotten it himself.*

Then she saw him.

He was pounding savagely at the controls of an airlock. He crouched and breathed heavily, both from the run itself and from its effect on Quindy's toe-job.

*Don't know if I can hold enough air to last the jump.* He forced hyperventilation. *Damn this panel! Why won't it—there!*

The airlock cycled open. He clambered inside and punched his wristcomm. "Geb. Are you close enough to read me?"

*"Firm. Right outside Airlock Seventeen. I've got our airlock open and Ash is waiting inside with oxygen. The*

*sooner we get out of here the better."*

"Pos. Though I bet my old pal Cuw called the attack off." *Here goes.*

Ahamkara saw the hatch cycling shut. In one burst of speed, she rushed forward, hit the deck and rolled under the dropping hatch. She made it inside.

All except her left foot.

The hatch slammed with crushing force against her ankle. Her fingers spasmed and lost their grip on the stopper. Eks had already turned around at the sound of her entry. He was staring at her in shock when she screamed.

"Shit!" he cried. *The lock won't cycle with the hatch wedged open!* He reached over to cycle the hatch all the way open. A voice yelled through the crack.

"Casualty there! Someone's foot."

*Great. Damage control.*

He found the controls to blow the hatch's explosive bolts. Following the instructions, he triggered the automatic sequencer. Footsteps neared the airlock.

"What're you *doing!*" Ahamkara screamed.

"What's it look like? I'm blasting my way out of here. *Eris* is right outside. I jump, we redshift."

"Ten seconds," said a courteous warning voice.

"You're leaving me to die! You bastard! You slicing gratshit *bastard!*" Tears and dirt smeared her makeup into a pitiable mask of hopeless rage that almost blotted the pain in her leg.

Eks flipped his fingers. *"You* followed *me,* clumsy." He breathed heavily.

"Five seconds."

"Hey," a voice in the tunnel shouted. "The bolts're gonna blow!"

"Four."

*"Please,* Marek! *Don't!"*

"Three."

Eks looked at her, his head swimming from hyperoxia. "Shit!" he cried furiously, jamming one hand into a pocket. "Two."

He pulled out a cutting laser, flicked it on, and angrily slashed the beam through the thinnest portion of her leg—right above the ankle.

"One."

"I hope you appreciate this, asshole." He lifted her up and grasped her delicate waist.

Ahamkara Tsadi stared at the blood pulsing from her footless ankle, and fainted.

"Contact."

*Wonderful,* Eks thought, grasping her tighter and seizing a strap with his other hand. He opened his jaws wide. His trachea and Eustachian tubes needed to remain open to equalize the pressure. *It has to work.* He had seen the feat or trick once in a holodrama. The script was from the ancient named Klarke, whom Eks knew had been a good and careful writer. *He knew what he was talking about, didn't he?*

The thundering roar of the explosive bolts and the escaping atmosphere lasted only as long as the air to carry the sound. The blast of wind from the sudden venting threatened to drag Eks and his burden into space. He let the air whistle out of his lungs and held fast.

Air whistled out of another chamber of his body, much to his surprise. *That wasn't in the holo I saw!* He was grateful that there was no other air to carry the sound.

His eyes burned as moisture boiled away from them in the vacuum. He saw the blown hatch tumble toward *Eris,* bounce off, and fly wide. All without a sound. The lighted airlock lay open a few dozen meters away. From one open airlock into another, through the vacuum of space without a spacesuit! (Already he was aware that Ahamkara Tsadi weighed precisely nothing.)

*Theba—keep your greedy damn' hands off me!*

He kicked to impart a modified jet effect to his body.

For an instant he floated with the weightless Ahamkara as if he were a holodrama or illobook superhero, sans skinTites. His empty lungs inhaled dry vacuum and exhaled damp vacuum in a vain attempt to circulate oxygen.

The airlock grew closer, wider.

Halfway across, he realized that he'd miscalculated his kick. He was drifting toward a portion of the hull a few meters aft of the lock. And the whole operation was supposed to be swift, swift; a matter of a second or three.

*This,* he mused with hypoxic giddiness, *is far too droll a way to die.*

He hit the cyprium hull using Ahamkara's body as a cushion. His clouding eyes glazed, gazed about for something to lash some fingers to. Some purchase. Anything. Red noise pounded inside his head. His arm flopped about in an effort to snag something—anything—before he bounced off and drifted away from the spacer and any possible chance of survival. It had become remote enough already, that possibility.

A strut gouged his palm, though the tingling fingers were beyond pain. He grabbed and pulled.

The longitudinal strut ended a meter this side of the airlock. Gripping it with one hand, he grasped Ahamkara's wrist with the other and used the strut as a pivot to swing her around toward the hatch.

She flipped in toward the lock. Releasing his grip on the strut, he allowed the newser's momentum to drag him after her. Inside. He'd made it!

*Never fear, Eks is . . .*

Before he could finish the thought or find and actuate the airlock controls, Marekallian Eks drifted into painless unconsciousness.

•   •   •

"Spacer *Eris* is moving away, sir."

*The bastard made it!* Captain Kukavi ran a hand over his glistening scalp. "Wait until it's moved out to a safe distance . . . and beam it into slag."

"Uh—"

"*Slag,* boy."

"Firm, sir."

*No slipsuckin' graverobber's going to play the traitor and get away!* Kukavi smiled. "Any other Orcas left with functioning DS?"

"About a dozen, sir."

The tattooed man nodded with satisfaction. "Excellent, Travkah. Have as many as possible lock on to *Eris* and await my signal."

The DSer obeyed.


"Musla's withered zork," Geb said, watching the screen. He maneuvered *Eris* past one Orca class dreadnought and watched its beamers rotate slowly to track him. "Are other ships locked on to us?"

"Yes." The computer answered quickly. "Nine functioning Orcas have a clear beamline to us. They will hold fire until we are far enough away that our destruction won't interfere with rescue operations."

"Just great." The small man punched up the inship comm. "Ash—have you got him?"

*"Cycling now. He didn't make it to the controls, but I'll have him revived in no time."*

"Ash—" His voice caught for an instant. "I'm going to have to jam it. They're tracking us and I know Kukavi. I know what he'll do."

Ashtaru was silent for a long time. *"He's coming around, Geb. He dragged Tsadi along. She's got to be put in the shipdoc."*

"Let her go."

*"Geb! He must've brought her along for a reason. I need two minutes is all."*

"Pos. I'm telling SIPACUM to ram us at the first sign of attack. Hear that, big boy?"

"Firm," the computer said. "Photons from plasma weapons will arrive before the ions. Upon detection, ship will go to defeat infinity instantaneously."

Geb swallowed hard. "Right, right."

*"Geb!"* Eks's voice rasped from the comm with pained effort. *"No jam-cram. Use the slipfield!"*

"Right, boss!" Geb shouted. In his eagerness to carry out Eks's startling order, he made a time-wasting error. He slapped the slipfield switches to power them up. Only then did he reach over to remove the jam-cram cassette from SIPACUM.

He lived to regret the error.

"Target spacer is at safe distance." The young man awaited his captain's command.

"Beam it." Kukavi spoke the order bitterly. He felt no savory delight in destroying his former ally. It was just something that had to be done.

Nine bolts of blue-white energy blazed toward *Eris*. In the instant it took for the ionized blobs to reach it, the spacer had vanished from the universe.

# 19

By some process I still don't quite understand, the problem had switched over to being a moral issue rather than one of the purely tactical ones I was used to dealing with. I felt insecure on this new territory. . . . How was I to know what was right and what was wrong . . . by what miraculous process?
From a purely practical point of view, how does destroying one's enemy help the victim? How could destruction bring justice—whatever it was—when destruction was the problem in the first place?

—J. Neil Schulman

*It worked again!* Trafalgar Cuw thought, releasing Quindy from his grasp. "That's it," he said, switching off the comm. "Let's go."

"Now we only have to worry about this fleet." Quindy glanced at SIPACUM. *Still looking for a SPOSE.*

Minutes passed. *Sunmother* boosted slowly past wreckage and other debris. Quindy stared emotionlessly at a mangled, bloated corpse of a woman that drifted across their field of view.

"Peacekeepers," she muttered. She turned to Trafalgar Cuw. "Are you or aren't you?" she asked.

"Am I or ain't I what?"

"TGO."

*My first time around, I asked questions. Amazing what*

*a little living and a dash of dying does to one's curiosity.*
He smiled. And said nothing.

"*Where are we headed?*" Kalahari commed from her
cabin. Her voice possessed an odd restlessness.

Trafalgar picked up the mike. "I sort of thought we'd
wait until we hit the Tachyon Trail before deciding. Hop
around a bit until we choose."

"*Any chance of hopping back to Terasaki?*"

"Yes," Quindy said over Trafalgar's shoulder. She nodded emphatically to her man. He nodded back, and winked.

Sweetface piped in from its DS station. "*Any hunches
as to Janja's whereabouts,* Myrzha *Cuw-san?*"

"I think we're getting closer to her all the time. Maybe
we should spend some time on a safe planet such as, oh . . ."
He paused as if mulling over a choice. "Oh, say maybe
. . . Franji. Or Thebanis. Pos—how about Thebanis?"

Quindy rolled her eyes. *What are we in for* now?

SIPACUM buzzed.

"Fifteen seconds," the man from Outreach said. "Say
goodbye to the Void."

Sweetface's voice: "Goodbye, Void."

"And good riddance!"

With that Captain Quindarissa took one last look at the
remains of the fleet on her 'puter simulation. Here and there,
tiny rescue boats flitted about the dead hulks of the Orcas.
Larger ships used tractors and repellors to clear debris. In
the darkness of the Carnadyne Void, only a few ships provided illumination for the unaided eye. Most work was done
with the aid of enhanced TP-puter images.

A sinking, falling, collapsing sensation enveloped her.
*Sunmother* converted to tachyons. Behind her in the Carnadyne Void, she left a thought.

The Gray Organization (Quindy presumed) had touched
that fleet with its shadowy hand. What would that hand do
if it ever touched her? Or one of the Satana Coalition? She

looked at Trafalgar Cuw. *Or . . . have we already been touched?*

HReenee's body heat rose even higher than its normal 40 degrees. She was on a ship that had *killed!* A spacer that had destroyed dozens of spacecraft and slain thousands of Galactics. Her vision remained sharp despite the emotions roaring through her body.

Every flare of light exploding from the target spacers had lanced through her like a slicer. She envisioned the destruction onboard the dreadnoughts—panic, chaos, fire, blood. *Blood!*

She gazed at her hands. The single claw in either middle finger had extruded unconsciously. She studied them closely. Beautiful curved talons. She slashed playfully at the viewing port as if she were tearing out the guts of the spacers with her own hands. She smiled.

Her skin tingled. The hairs all over her arms and legs and back prickled up. She floated on a hot, trembling river of excitement that even the discomfort of tachyon conversion had not abated.

The killer ship had left far behind it the devastated Horde and enough surviving witnesses to ensure that rumors of the awesome power of TGO would continue to spread. Retellings of the story would increase the number of attackers from invisibility to a counter-fleet of ridiculous proportions. What else could so nearly have obliterated such a mighty host?

(The survivors would thank Musla or Booda or Gri or a score of other gods for their good fortune. Few would consider that—just maybe—their lives were not so important to their gods as they were *un*important to TGO. No one liked to ponder its own personal insignificance.)

HReenee felt abundantly significant. She had fallen in with *killers*. Sanctioned killers. Legal killers. A shadow agency that made (or prevented!) history through the enlightened application of death. An *effective* peacekeeping force.

She walked to the con with sensual strides. Every turn brought her body in sleek, stroking contact with corners, stanchions, furnishings, hardware. She stepped into the con-cabin in such a way as to drag an arm with languorous delicacy across the hatch's edge. She stood proudly erect, noting with pleasure that her eight nipples were doing so, too. She felt a flaming heat in her loins and a primitive lust in her soul.

"Yao," she said softly.

Ratran and Janja both turned to see her. Janja *cherm*ed HReenee's emotions and stiffened.

"I'm going to get some rest," she said. "All this murder's taken a lot out of me."

She looked coolly at the HRal on her way out. *You've gotten what you wanted, HReenee. And you'll find out only too soon that it's exactly what Rat wants, too.*

HReenee and Ratran stood alone in the con-cabin. She moved close to him. The pupils of her yellow-gold eyes widened.

Yao's expressionless black eyes gazed back.

She touched a shoulder to his. "I want to join you. I want to be on your next assignment." She rubbed against him and spoke in a low, throaty pitch that was very nearly a purr. "I want to help you kill."

In her cabin, Janja lay quietly on her bed and stared blankly at the walls. Though they sped toward Kebri Dahir, her thoughts remained in the Void. She saw *Sunmother* boosting away from her again and again.

*I passed my friends on the way to destroy the Enemy. I was so efficient, so loyal to TGO that I passed them without a word. I was on the trail of the Enemy.*

*And when I reached the Enemy, my friends were right there with them.*

She rolled over and tried to suppress the tears building up in her eyes. Her clothes felt restrictive, painful to her flesh. She wanted to rip them from her and leave it all behind. TGO, Ratran, the spaceways. She knew she wouldn't. Couldn't. She was Janja of The Gray Organization.

And... No One Left TGO.

*Traf,* her thoughts cried out, aching to be heard across the parsec abyss. *Quindy, Cinnabar, Hellfire. I miss you all. Even you, Sweetface, even you.*

Again the thought plagued her. *What were they doing with the fleet? With the Enemy? Rat tells me to kill and I kill. I might have killed my friends. If Rat labels someone an Enemy, does that make it so? Is the friend of an enemy also an enemy?*

She buried her face in the pillow. Soft white hair filled the depression around her, covering her.

*Why does everything called "bad" in this universe seem to be mixed up with "good?" And why does there seem to be no "good" that remains pure, untainted by the "bad?"*

*Am I good because Ratran Yao tells me I'm good? Am I evil because I do evil things?* Her chest quivered with weak sobs. *Can I really be both? Am I doing good for many by doing evil to a few?* She trembled with fury. *If I am doing that, then Jonuta aided this greater good by performing the minor evil of enslaving me!*

Fists slammed against the amorphous mattress. *NO! I'll never believe logic so hideous. Never!*

Janjaheriohir of Aglaya wept for only a moment. She exerted psychocytological control over her breathing, her tears, and her shaking. She sat up on the bed.

*Good and evil are what I decide them to be. No one else*

*can make the choice for me. Not Jonuta, nor Corundum,
not Ratran Yao.*

*I was forced to join TGO. I was ordered to kill. I was
assigned to draw others into the fold. I can see the evils.*

*I can also see the good. And that is what I'll serve. The
good that I see. No one can steal that vision from me.*

Captain Kukavi gazed at the remains of his fleet, at the
ruination of his glorious vision, stolen from him in a few
blinding instants by nameless, faceless invaders.

*Betrayed by someone inside,* he thought. *Someone high
up. I wouldn't be surprised if it were Eks. He seemed to
know that other Outie.*

The recovery of the injured and trapped had taken several
days-ess. The living placed the dead in the holds of an
unsalvageable Orca.

There was something about a burial in space that disturbed Kukavi. Totally apart from the death that necessitated
it, casting bodies into the achingly limitless parsec abyss
conjured up an image of eternity too sobering even for the
cold sober Captain Kukavi.

To abandon thousands of dead in the void of the Void
so poetically approached his own personal concept of Hell
that he found it difficult to preside over the simple cere-
monies.

He floated in his white mlss a few hundred meters from
the funeral spacer. Hundreds of others drifted nearby in a
null-G cluster of bereavement. He switched on his comm
and recited a blessing for the Dead. He had recited it often
before this day, and he had no doubt that he would repeat
it again and again until the day it was spoken for him.

"'Unto them from whose eyes the veil of life hath fallen
may there be granted the accomplishment of their true
Wills.'" He coughed to cover a catch in his voice. "'Whether
they will absorption in the Infinite, or to be united with

THE CARNADYNE HORDE    189

their chosen and preferred, or to be in contemplation, or to be at—to be at *peace,* or to achieve the labor and heroism of incarnation on this planet or another, or in any Star, or aught else—unto them may there be granted the accomplishment of their Wills.'" He coughed again.

"We lost a lot a few days ago," he said in a quiet, firm voice. "Some of us lost everything. But we who... well, we who're still alive have a chance. I wouldn't blame any of you if you decided to pack it all in and go home. But those of you who think this fight is worth winning shouldn't give up hope. Hope may be all we have at the moment, but in it we can find the strength to rebuild.

"The Council took the precaution of constructing a hideout eight thousand light-years above the plane of the Galaxy. Maybe we'll be just as vulnerable there as here, or maybe we'll be considered too far away to cause trouble. Any who choose to join us can get a special SIPACUM cassette onboard *Liberator* after security clearance.

"We'll set the boosters now, and have a few minutes of silence."

Kukavi pressed a stud on his wrist controls to actuate the cemetery ship's few operational boosters. They flared briefly, nudging the dreadnought away from the rest of the Horde.

It would drift slowly for years, until repeated collisions with dust and micrometeroids reduced its velocity to that of matter within the Void. There it would rest for eternity.

Unless something bigger or faster chanced to hit it.

Kukavi returned to *Liberator* and the final preparations for departure from the Void.

The remnants of the fleet dispersed. Some returned to the spaceways; others followed *Liberator* to Retreat. In a few hours, nothing remained of the Carnadyne Horde but some twisted wreckage and a bitter memory to haunt those who had escaped alive.

Yet life stirred in the Carnadyne Void.

Thousands of kloms away from the shattered armada flared the boosters of a sleek, compact spacer. Cautiously, warily, Tura ak Saiping edged toward the drifting hulks. Her DS computer kept careful watch for intruders.

The dorsal hatch in the midsection of *Black Dawn* slid open. Five spherical cybers shot out and boosted toward the nearest dreadnought.

She scanned the spacer for life, firmed that there was no one to interfere, and began her own salvage operation. Unlike members of the Horde, she was in no hurry.

Tura ak Saiping suspected that TGO had orchestrated the attack on this fleet. And while she had vowed vengeance upon The Gray Organization in her hate, she was not averse to profiting from its *faits accomplis*. She guided the machines in their search for booty.

*I pick through graveyards now, Randy, so that I might someday find the means to avenge you. Or join you.*

A cyber signaled her. She gazed at the computer simulation. It had recovered a small missile, undetonated, from the drifting wreckage near the Orca.

She ordered the cyber to bring it back to *Black Dawn*— carefully. The potent weapon intrigued her. *If it's still functional, it might just be engraved someday with the name of Sinchung Sin.*

Tura ak Saiping worked slowly, methodically. Her cybers picked through the broken fleet for weeks, until she had found enough material to fill not only her spacer's cramped holds, but every cable-tow on its hull.

When *Black Dawn* departed the Carnadyne Void, it looked like a clump of scraggly kudzu set adrift along the spaceways.

# Epilog

"No, Geb!" Marekallian screamed with his bleeding lungs.

The blinding flash of light from the nine ion beams gave
way to a sickening wrench. Eks was certain that he had died
right then. It took him an instant to realize that he was still
thinking. In that instant, the agony seized him.

Geb had been unable to power up Eks's slipfield in time.
The ship had jam-crammed as programmed. They had gone
Forty Percent City.

Transition to "subspace" was a touchy business. Finding
a safe point of entry took time. To *ram* a ship without
warning into transition phase was more than dangerous—
it could be deadly.

The probability of a ship's surviving a jam-cram intact
(with or without unspecified damage) was a non-terminat-
ing, non-repeating 59.7731-and-so-on-to-infinity per cent.
That left a 40.2269 (et cetera) per cent chance of . . . something
else. Where the losers of such a gamble went was anybody's
guess—and few liked to venture such guesses.

The legendary pirate Artisune Muzuni had gone Forty
Percent City. So had the sorely missed brothel-owner Ga-
nesa. Kislar Jonuta's enemy Corundum had jam-crammed
to save his life, never to be seen again.

And now, to his horror, the fate of Marekallian Eks and his crew rested upon the cruel, impartial mathematics of probability.

The universe thundered around Eks. Pain racked through every nerve ending in his body. Gemlike colors of piercing intensity cut through him. A violent falling sensation pulled him downward into the sucking mouth of a voracious monstrosity.

Suddenly he saw himself from every possible point of view. Every atom of his being was open to him. He reached for his heart and crushed it.

He screamed for eternity. The universe unfolded for him, withered and collapsed. All the vicious brutality of creatures throughout time and space slashed through him in an instant of unimaginable torment.

*This is it,* he thought. *This is the death we fear and avoid. This is our "peace unutterable!"* He marveled at the ability of his thoughts to transcend his nervous system's devastation. He felt an awful splitting take place—mind from body, thought from feeling. He was two, now. Separate and distinct yet still bound up in one being.

A vast emptiness surrounded him. He drifted through a roaring silence that foretold the end of all *things*. It mattered not to him.

Marekallian Eks gazed upon the face of the Dark Universe and felt no fear.

*I am beyond death now.* A calm enveloped him. The terror finally made sense. *Birth, life, death. Eternal. The individual is vital to the endless cycle, yet is meaningless to the whole. I spent my life battling a force that is as nothing compared to the universe.*

In a blazing explosion of awareness, Marekallian found his purpose, his final goal. He knew what had to be done.

His thoughts made a sudden departure. *How are the others?* He tried to visualize *Eris*.

He saw it as if from outside. It drifted through the Dark Universe, lost. It might stay there forever. Or . . .

Eks lay in the airlock, staring up blankly. The oxygen mask Ashtaru had slipped over his mouth and nose still rested in place. Spatters of blood coated the inside of the clear plas, leaking out around the edges where it touched his face. He breathed slowly, steadily.

Ashtaru lay at the foot of the cyberdaktari. Her face rested in a puddle of her own illness. The odor awakened her. With great care, woozy and nauseated, she sat up and leaned against the shipdoc.

Inside the medical repair/resuscitation unit lay the wounded newser. The cyber's efforts to revive Tsadi and regenerate her missing foot had ben interrupted by the jam-cram. It ran a self-monitor on its circuits, pronounced itself functional, and resumed work on its patient.

Geb stared without comprehension at the controls. He was certain that he had seen *Eris* sundered by impossible forces. SIPACUM, however, reported that *only* about seventy per cent of the ship's systems were damaged. Life support still functioned inside most of the spacecraft.

*We've survived!*

He took a deep breath of *Eris*'s air and set to work. He would worry about the rest of the crew as soon as he was certain that the ship was secure.

Klyjil bazRakava had the worst headache he could remember. Worse even than the one upon being revived from his cryosphere. He stumbled out of his sweat-soaked chair and onto the deck.

His cabin seemed frighteningly odd to him. Angles of perception twisted to the pains in his head. He lay still for a moment, grasping for any strength that might be left inside him.

*This was jam-cram.* His first coherent thought was followed swiftly by another. *I survived!*

The Akil tried to stand up, found that he was too weak. On hands and knees he crawled out of his cabin, pausing at intervals to rest or merely to breath. A few meters down the tunnel, he summoned the strength to stand. Long delicate fingers grasped a stanchion firmly. Lean muscles pulled him slowly up. Even in the spacer's light gravity, the act required supreme effort. He looked around him.

Anything that had not been battened down had been strewn through the spacer like leaves in a storm. Sheets, utensils, electronics, edutapes, vials of encephaloboosts, 'puterfaxes spilled out of cabins and holds into the tunnel.

Klyjil walked with careful steps toward the con-cabin.

The constant vibration of the aircon had ceased. That, he realized, accounted for the deadly quiet of the ship. He passed an airlock. The light breathing inside caught his attention. Peering in, he saw the Mindrunner breathing weakly and staring upward with unseeing eyes. Klyjil crouched over the Galactic's body and examined him carefully.

Eks's raven hair lay in limp wet clumps against his scalp. His skin was moist, clammy. Only his autonomic systems seemed to be functioning.

*Not dying. Stable, perhaps. Any others alive?* He found the intraship comm, punched it on.

"Can anyone hear me?" he asked in a hesitant voice.

*"Klyjil,"* Geb's voice possessed a softness that surprised the Akil. *"If you're well enough, please check on Ashtaru and Marek. I'm trying to get* Eris *back together."*

"Yes, Geb," he replied. "Marek is in the airlock. Unconscious, but alive. Where are we?"

*"I don't know."* Geb paused for a long moment, busy with other matters. *"Take him to the shipdoc. Ashtaru should be there."*

"I am, Geb." Ashtaru's voice sounded distant and weary. *"I—I think I've fractured my arm. Tsadi's in the daktari now. She's alive."*

*"Big deal. You two get up here when you've taken care of Marek and we'll get started on repairs."*

Klyjil lifted Marek's arms to drag him out of the airlock. The Galactic made no sounds of pain or awareness. The Akil moved slowly with his burden. In the tunnel he spread out a sheet and laid the body on it. Dragging the sheet proved much easier. Even so, he took nearly half an hour to reach the medical bay.

Ashtaru scrubbed her face with a few alcohol prep-pads and injected a full exodermic syringe of endorphinol and Stand-up into her arm. She looked at Klyjil and Marekallian.

Sweat and grime plastered the Akil's fur against his skin. The beautiful, sensual creature looked like an abused and frightened animal. His large, golden eyes gazed sadly at hers as he deposited Eks before her.

She wanted to cry. Instead, she knelt unsteadily beside the unconscious man and checked him over with a portable scanner.

*Pupillary responses normal. Blood pressure and pulse both low but steady. Breathing steady.*

*No brainwave pattern.*

She slumped against the cool white side of the cyber-daktari and hung her head.

"Coma."

With Klyjil's help, she moved the body to a bed and covered it up to the shoulders. At her direction, Klyjil removed the oxygen mask and wiped away the blood crusted on Marek's face.

Klyjil set Ashtaru's arm in a plasticast and walked with her to the con-cabin.

Geb tried to oversee a dozen separate diagnosis programs at once. *Eris* had held together through the jam-cram. Barely. They had returned to "normal" space. But where?

"Maybe this is what happens to most of them that go Forty Percent City." Ashtaru sat in the navigator's chair, watching SIPACUM try to find a familiar star. "They wind up in an unexplored portion of the Galaxy."

"We're safe, at least, wherever we are. For the time being." *I wish Marek were here.*

Geb felt a cold pain shoot through him at the thought that his captain—the man who had rescued him from slavery, however inadvertently—might never waken. He was stable, and most comas were reversible. Still, technology had its limits. Memories destroyed could not be retrieved (and Marekallian Eks was not the sort to carry a memory-corder). Personality, once obliterated, would never be the same a second time.

*Wish he was here.*

Geb had no way of knowing that he was.

Marekallian Eks looked over his comatose body and left the sickbay. His *sense of perception* shifted to the con-cabin. He *watched* Ashtaru and Klyjil assist Geb in checking and repairing *Eris*'s damage. He *felt* satisfied that they were safe. He would never lose track of them, as long as they kept the empty shell of his body alive.

*Right now, though, I have something to attend to.*

Marekallian Eks, Mindrunner, let his mind run, let it race away from *Eris* and his friends. He directed his will toward his chosen destination.

No one on *Eris* noted his departure.

(Someone did, thousands of parsecs away. The Iceworld Connection noticed a disturbance at the periphery of the Dark Universe . . . but was too busy to bother with such an unimportant fluctuation. Carnadyne returned to her experiments. If this field could be generated around an individual and maintained even against the vacuum . . . why, a person could actually leap from one ship to another without a space-suit and without adverse effect. Still, the thousand-year flower was about to go into its blooming cycle, something never seen by human eyes—or, in Carnadyne's case, al-most-human, once-human eyes. The air-maintenance field was not nearly so important, and would wait. . . .)

• • •

"I have no fix so far on any catalogued star." Ashtaru chewed her lip while she tapped another command into SIPACUM. "It'll take a while to I.D. a galaxy or quasar. We *can't* be so far away that the rest of the *universe* is unidentifiable!"

"Can't we?" Geb said cheerlessly.

Of the three, only Klyjil bazRakava ventured no opinion or guess as to their whereabouts. Neither Geb nor Ashtaru expected him to.

The point was that Klyjil/Phoenix didn't have to guess. He recognized the surrounding star systems. The two Galactics had no idea that they were only a few hundred light-years from Kuzih: the five-world confederation that had dispatched Klyjil millennia before, as a probe/spy.

He had been set adrift in a cryosphere in the hope of being "found" by a spacefaring race. That never happened. He had drifted for ages and might have continued to do for more ages, if the cryosphere had not made autoplanetfall on Arepien. It was found and enshrined by the Galactic race that had settled there—before their collapse into "savagery."

Kuzih had sent out other spies before Klyjil, and he suspected that the others had been dispatched since. He had been found by Marekallian Eks—"Mindrunner" and grave-robber member of a race unknown to Kuzih at the time of Klyjil's freezing. He had no doubt that the Akil, Letii and Sisika still existed, and that more cryospheres had been released to spy on this "new" race.

If not, Klyjil had four specimens to bring home....

*Kuzih.* He shivered in anticipation and wished for a brush to groom his lightly furred body. He looked about. The damage to *Eris* was extensive enough that they would be stranded for days or weeks. That gave Klyjil bazRakava sufficient time to think of a plan.

*Kuzih!*

# SPECIAL SUPPLEMENT:
## SLANG ALONG THE SPACEWAYS

Slang comes and goes; slang changes and then changes again. Naturally plenty of slang, along with euphemisms and abbreviations, exists along the spaceways—far more than we translate in the novels! No use in letting a book run twice as long by leaving in *all* the profanity used by men in combat, or by all those who ply the parsec abyss of space.

It's death and dying, sex and sexing that yield the most euphemisms and slang expressions. "He was called" and "She passed over" small-town newspapers long said and probably still do, dodging, along with the "passed on" or "passed away." The Vietnam war yielded KIA (for "killed in action" but used orally as "he was KIA" or simply: Q: "Where's Willie?" and A: "KIA"). That war popularized "bought the farm," too—a euphemism for retired, as a euphemism for the ultimate retirement: *killed*. That yielded "The Sarge bought it" or "O Lord, I'm short—don't let me buy it now!" (Translation: "God, the length of time I have to stay here is almost over, so please don't let me get killed now!") The old "knock off" has become the shorter "to off," which means the same as "to blow away" and "to take him down"—to kill.

A Cuban dispatch about the murder of one pro-Cuban Grenadan leader by others stated that he should not have been "physically eliminated," and people do persist in using high-sounding phrases such as "executed" and "assassinated" to mean *murdered*—presumably because *murder* is an ugly word.

Eighteenth Century pornography employed "pego/dart/ member/organ" to dodge the word "penis," and "quim/quiff/ Garden of Venus/Gates of Paradise" and lots more to mean "vagina," among other dodges. Those gave way to "dick/ prick/ dong/whang" and worse, along with the now overused *cock*. Usually such popularization unto overuse presages a change to a new euphemism. When an expression for dying or the coital organs or act becomes widely used, others "have to" be invented.

(Consider all the dodging involved in this progression(?): "boneyard→graveyard→cemetery→memorial garden.")

More than a decade ago "Let's blow this damn' joint" became "Let's split this fuckin' place." The former adjective means no more than the latter; it's just a word. The common, widespread use of that old four-letter word for coitus surely makes us overdue for another "forbidden" one—four-letter or otherwise for the actual act. (The expression "sexual intercourse" long ago forced "social intercourse"—meaning *conversation*—right out of the language!) Surely the substitute isn't just "effing" from "f__ing." We'll see. Bet on it that the next war will bring with it new derogatory slang for the Other Side, and for being dead/dying—and probably for marijuana, too.

We come up with so many substitutes for expletives and curse- and cuss-words that we can't even remember what "dad-gummed" means. Among marvelous dodges I've heard are "Darn it to heck!" and "heckfire and dern-nation"—both from "nice" college girls who wouldn't cuss; and the "teed off" that my younger sister used when she got to college;

it replaced "peed off," which was short for "pissed off," which meant perturbed or angered. I've gotten away with calling someone a "sunday witch" just as little Japanese boys used to call out something along the lines of *"moddahokka sunnakabiki"* to GIs on R&R from Korea—and get away with it because the guys were laughing so hard.

What's a LEM? An LED? LCD? RADAR? S.O.B.? A muthah?

Here's a compendium of some of the slang and euphemisms used in the **Spaceways** books; not all of it, because who knows what new expression is going to turn up tomorrow on what planet?—or what a Jarp is *really* saying when its translation helmet (naturally shortened to "translahelm") says "flainin'" or "vug"?

A few of the expressions listed here aren't technically slang. They are abbreviations or euphemisms much used, and this is a good place to include them. Even "spacer" is a slang word, just as "car/gun/stereo/plane/laser" are slang expressions understood by all members of society—but not necessarily by members of another society!

The background notebooks for the **Spaceways** series are painfully thick and detailed—with lots of gaps, still. We've updated and detailed the (still inadequate) map, and provided a list of planets-suns-capitals-inhabitants in the 16th novel, *The Planet Murderer,* and here's some slang.*

—John Cleve, 1983

---

*Please don't ask for a list of all the people so far; at least four have been named Achmet and besides, half those flainers have been Poofed/placidated!

**ASP**   report: All Systems Pos(itive)

**ASRS**   report or request: All Sensors Report, Syncretized (various sensor readings combined for better understanding of object or situation)

**Barracuda**   a class of spaceship, used by TGW

**blastman**   a mining operation's explosions engineer

**blip-silhouettes**   on radar, for instance

**blue-lighted**   malfunctioned; blew out

**blueshift**   *v.* approach, come, arrive. From astronomical terminology (opp: *redshift*)

**BOOPFAITU**   Booda's Plan For All In The Universe—a "fact" to believers. Otherwise an *expl*(etive) or *swearby*, as in "BOOPFAITU! We *did* it!"

**brainboost**   *n.,v.* artificial enhancement of knowledge or mental power; hypnolearning; remification

**bug**   *n.* stupid ass, poor bastard. Used about as the overused XX Century "asshole," as in "Stop that bug before he fobs up everything!"

**bungle**   *n.* mess, bad trip: a negative. Also used as *expl.*

**burok**   bureaucracy or bureaucratic process. 2: *expl,* as "Crap!" or obscenity, as "What the burok do you think you're doing, you flainin' bug?"

**butsy**   *adj.* indicative of a well-developed rear. With one *b,* yes .

**butsy-busty**   *adj.* indicative of a woman who's got it all

**C!**   distress signal, as *Mayday!* meaning "Help I'm in trouble!" (see *CYR*)

**CAGS**   Computer And Guidance System

**CAGSVIC**   CAGS plus Vocally Interactive Computer unit

**cake**   a female; replaces "chick," with disrespectful overtones

**card**   *v.* pay, as in "I'll card for the drinks." See *loosecard*

**C! CYR!**   spaceship in trouble signal: We're being boarded *(Red Rovered)*

**celldye**   ("cytocosmetics") dye for skin, hair, or eyes that is ingested or injected, and colors at the cellular level. "Permanent" but readily reversible or changeable; *can* be for a predetermined length of time, after which color naturally reverts to natural

**chulwar**   a Ghanji animal. Extended to a mild derogatory (*derog*), usually preceded by "stupid"

**civserv**   *n.* a civil "servant"—guv employee: burok, jr. grade

**Cobs**   expl on Jorinne: "Cobs! What a mess!" as in "Good grief/Good lord"

**ComeBack Anytime Passes**   rainchecks, issued by bars, etc. onplanet or on(space)stations

**Cool Winds**   Aglayan farewell

**coper**   *n.* one who copes; probably invented by Frederick Perls, founder of Gestalt therapy/philosophy

**cork**   *n.* see *slicer*
   *v.* to slice/stuff/soar with, in a tryst

**cred**   *n.* money (stells, or stellar monetary units—currency)

**crosser**   AC-DC person or one who—like Janja, Shieda, Quindy, others—prefers heterosexuality but will switch-hit. Not applied to Jarps

**dam', damn'**   *adj:* damned. Since "damn" is a verb, it won't work as an *adjective* except by unedited know-littles.

**Dance**   when capitalized, this indicates stopper setting #2: neural jangler or traumatizer (see Freeze, Fry, Poof, Zap)

**day-ess**   *n.* day-standard: 25 hours

**de-esser**   DSer: Defense Systemry operator (gunner)

**deg**   *n.* ancient form of pornography involving the most common female phantasy, possession/"rape"—degradation. Also called *bodice ripper, historical romance*. Kenowa's favorite entertainment, after the real thing

**derog**   *n., adj.* a derogative; or *derogatory*

**demon**   Since **Spaceways** is eastern-based and gremlins are not, this is what glitches and snafus are blamed on.

**digger**   *n.* penis, on Sekhar (where the female counterpart is *oasis*)

**diplomish**   *n.* TGO slang: a "diplomatic mission" is a covert operation, often but not necessarily a wet job (*kill-mission*).

**down**   *n.* a bad scene; bummer. Also applied to such a person. See *downer*

**downer**   *n.* a down-bringer, as in "poison person" or Al Capp's Joe Bpftsplk

**drug-dreamer**    *n.* a bummish person who drugs too much (*narcobum*); may or may not be an addict, technically, but will do nigh anything for cred

**ecstat**    *adj.* high, on drugs or sex

**em-ess**    *n.* month-standard: thirty 25-hour days

**erozone**    erogenous zone

**excavator**    Sekhar again: frequent user of his digger: cocksman

**eyecorder**    camera. Develops instantly but stores rather than extrudes (which it will also do at the touch of a button)

**eyesystemry**    a ship's "eyes" or system of optical scanning devices

**fingerflip**    *n,v:* a flipping of the fingers; standard multi-meaning digital "shrug." ("Cup" all four fingers on thumb and "let" them snap forward as if sprung, rapidly but one by one, starting with the little finger)

**firm**    *v.* to confirm, as "Do you firm that?" "I firm that" or simply "Firm," meaning "double-Pos"

**flainer**    *derog.* S.O.B., jerk, or bastard come close, although the verb "to flain" does not properly exist

**flaining**    *adj., derog.* usually without the g. "Damned" or a mild form of "fuckin'" as adjective, meaning...dad-gummed?

**flash**    *n.,v.:* orgasm

**flasher**    *n.:* a very good lover, one way or another

**flash-spot**    *n.:* erozone, q.v.

**Full-House Distribution or -Syndrome**    Also "the Schwartz-Vik Conformation: the Jarp chromosomal distribution indicating male-female-hereditary (46XXXYYh. Yours is 46XX if you're female, 46XY if you're male. See **Spaceways #1**, page 53ff)

**flit**    *v.* to move through space, where one does not "fly"

**flit**    *n.* a spaceflight or jaunt

**flip five**    *v.* see *fingerflip*

**fob**    *v.* to bother, disturb, to fool or put on; to foul or mess up someone or something

**fobbed it**    fouled up/screwed up

**fobber**    *n.* a person who fouls up

**fobbies, screaming**   "Keep that up and you'll give me the screamin' fobbies!"

**fobbo(s)**   *n*. idiot; fobber; bug (q.v.)

**fobbo, screaming**   "That drove her into a screamin' fobbo!" (Not literally so)

**fobbo**   *adj*. crazy, either literally or otherwise. "She's fobbo" can mean simply "she's nuts" or have a more serious psychiatric application

**fobby**   *adj*. used as in "Don't get all shook/shook up about it"

**fradgitator**   see *frag:* a person (or thing) that is a real pain in the, er, neck

**frag**   *v*. to bother; to get on the nerves of: "You're starting to frag me with your constant idiotic use of 'basically,' man!"

**fragged**   *adj*. (or past tense of *frag*) torn to pieces emotionally, as in "shot all to hell"

**fraggy**   *adj*. the same

**Freeze**   when capitalized, this indicates stopper setting #1: a sort of loose rigidity/paralysis

**freshbaked**   *adj*. for *cake:* a virgin

**Fry**   when capitalized, stopper setting #3 (barrel #2), also called "Poof." Death by disintegration/carbonization—a form of killing that cleans up after itself. There's a lot of this going around, along the spaceways

**furbag**   *derog*. from Mott-chindi ("Macho") adapted by Hellfire. *Probably* derived from a mangy grat. See *furbagging*

**furbagging**   *adj*. "Get that furbaggin' thing out of here!" A meaningless mildly derogatory adjective

**gerbolansk**   *derog*. literally, a bioengineered horse-plus, beast of burden

**glued**   *adj*. unfobbied; together; has head on straight

**grabbles**   *expl*. the spacefarer's "gosh" or "holy mackerel," since not everybody cusses (never mind that "Gee" and "Gosh" both come from "God!")

**grat**   *expl*. literally a dog-sized animal

**grick**   *expl*. origin unknown. "He's a real grick" might mean schmuck, downer, jerk

**grickhead**    variant of *grick,* indicating a possible relationship to excrement

**grotch**    *v.* to kvetch or grouch at, as in "Oh, stop grotching."

**grunje**    *derog.* spreading from Jorinne; a drag, a schmuck, jerk, mild S.O.B.

**grunjok**    *n.* a fluffy bioengineered dog-cat favored by the wealthy. Sour in disposition, and so a *derog.*

**"Grunt?"**    a spoken word, meaning "Huh?" or "What?" See *Uh*

**guideline**    *n.,v.* order or command, stemming from "Today's new OSHA guideline stipulates that... (or else)." Extended to "We guideline you to stop/You are guidelined to halt."

**guv-clerk**    originally, the inventer of *guideline* as command. Any minor burok or "official," anywhere. Usually officious. It thinks it has authority—if it thinks, or can think, which is seldom the case.

**Holy Prophet!**    *expl.* Muslim swearby; *real* adherents add a blessing on the Prophet

**hour-standard**    a slip. Hours, mins, secs are standard among all Galactics. Days, weeks, months and years of course vary from planet to planet. A day-ess (day-standard) is 25 hours, that having been discovered as best or most comfortable to the most humans/Galactics. That doesn't help if you're a farmer on a planet with a 20- or 27½-hour rotation

**hotcha district**    the wild bar-and-red light district in every spaceport town, close to the shuttleport

**hoy!**    "Hey!" as in "Hoy, jacko!" meaning "Hey, mac!"

**humongerous**    *adj.* proper spelling of "humongous" before American miseducation. Means big or bigger than that, depending on who's talking about what, and when. And where

**hunstell**    an anachronism for 100 stells (stellar monetary units) or a 100-stell note; it is properly decistell(s)

**hust**    *n.* specifically a prostitute, for money. Extended as derog, naturally

**icing licker**    distinctly bigoted term for cunnilinguist or female homosexual

**ignite**  to turn on anything (engine) and as slan𝗀. to arouse a person, sexually

**IRS**  *n*. theft by lie or intimidation; origin unknown

**IRS**  *v*. to steal, as in "appropriate" or "confiscate" or by state intimidation

**jacko**  guy (of either sex) Used as "mac/buddy/fella/bucko/ jack"

**jam-cram**  *v*. to slam a spacecraft into tachyon conversion (and thus flit *ftl* for faster-than-light) without regard for safety; e.g.: without awaiting puter report on what might be nearby to fob or destroy the ship/crew/systems

**jinkle**  *v*. used as "tinker's dam"; "It's not worth a jinkle/I can't see worth a j"

**joc**  *v*. to kid, joke; usually "joc around"

**key out**  *v*. to end one's watch or turn at the controls (oncon) of a spacer. Not the same as *log off*

**knobbles**  *n*. breasts, infrequently. See *warheads*

**lacer**  a laser-beam cutter; also *lace-cutter*

**lamprey**  *n*. computer traumatizer described in **Spaceways** #3-180. Attaches itself to spacer hull and *bonds* there, molecularly—while it "lies" to SIPACUM, which becomes undependable

**liftplate**  *n*. elevator floor—with or without walls

**loosecard**  *n*. free spender; good-time Charlie who's loose with his credcard (q.v.)

**makhseem**  *n*. used by the Akil of Kuzih and so known to few; it is such a nice and lovely act that they would not translate it as *fornicate*. Humans would

**Matana's Mistake**  doesn't belong here, really. Planetbound physicist Matana, *long* ago, "proved" that far fewer stars existed than were supposed, and that inhabited and even habitable planets were even less likely. The poor bug died a laughing stock.

**meld**  *n.*, *v*. replaces zipper; may be nevelcro or field-bonded

**mlss**  *n*. pronounced "molss": mobile life support system. A spacesuit

**mod**  *n*. room in a hotel—or oftener, a karavansery

**modified stopper**  the **Spaceways** troublemaker. Its recta-boosted #2 setting is Zap, rather than Dance: it induces immediate unconsciousness. Also called Outworld stopper; Outer planet stopper; rectaboosted-2 stopper

**mumsy** *n.* old woman; also derog as in "Oh, don't be a mumsy!" (spoilsport)

**mufper** *n.* pronounceable acronym for multi-functional-personal beam-sidearm: the official designation for *stopper*

**muth** *n.* motherly woman, old woman—not derog

**Myrzha** Arabic "mister" (as is suffixed "seety"); Terasaks and others use -*san*

**narcobum** drug-user, usually jobless and likely dangerous; not necessarily an addict

**needler** *n.* a misnomer; it's a tranqer "gun" that spits a skin-penetrating dose *without* a needle

**neg** short for negatory: "No"

**negatory** "No"; see *neg*

**nipped** caught by policers

**nipper** onplanet policer: a cop

**oasis** Sekhar's term for vagina. Also a popular term for bar or lounge

**ob** *n.* *obligation*, plus. A favor on call from someone you "have an ob on" or who "owes you an ob." Jonuta holds a bunch of obs on various people on varous worlds, and uses them as trade items. Kalahari/Hellfire has accepted an ob from all other members of the Satana Coalition.

**Oh shit** without the comma, yes. Sort of an inside joke with the Satana Coalition. Cinnabar might well greet Janja with it. See *wonderful*

**off-commed** cut off the commbox or commlink: broke off communicating ("hung up")

**oncon** *adj.* When a spacefarer has the con(trol console) duty in the con-cabin of a ship, it is *oncon*—*it* being the ancient either-sex pronoun.

**plas** plastic, in combination or alone

**plasmer** common name for a plasma-hurling pulsar beamer/ weapon

**plass** plastic tumbler—a lot better than those snappable hand-cutters in so many hotels/motels!

**pod** any container, from small pak to ship's external cargo-hauling "crate"

**Payday!** *expl.* usually a substitute for a happy/exuberant "Gosh!" or "Wow!"

**pilgrim** a follower or "walker" of the Way: a Taoist

**placidate** *v.* to take out, off, remove, take down, Poof: to kill

**pleascenter** erozone (q.v.)

**policer** *n.* unisex term for police or policeman/-woman—neither of which word is used along the spaceways other than as the verb "to police"

**poof** to get rid of anything in a molecular converter/garbage disposall

**Poof** when capitalized, to kill, esp. with stopper setting #3: Fry

**poofer** *n.* garbage can that never has to be emptied! Everyplace has one or more of these molecular disintegrators/reclaimers-and-recyclers.

**pos** short for *pository* or positive: Yes. "Yes" still exists.

**purple heebie, screamin' fobbies** originating in drug-use, this phrase has been extended, as in "You pop your knuckles one more time and I'm gonna go into a purple heebie!"

**recs** recommendations

**rectaboosted** *adj.* extra strength; as stopper setting Two (see *modified stopper*)

**red out** *v.* pass into partial unconsciousness, as opposed to *black out*

**redshift** *v.* go, depart, leave. From astronomical terminology (opp: *blueshift*)

**Red Rover** *n., v.* boarding in space, usually by bad guys. See *C!* signal

**relief corner** sitter (restroom or pissoir)

**riser** *n.* ah, the vagaries of slang! On Jorinne, this is a downer, a bug

**sadiki** *n.* Arabic for moonshine whiskey—literally "my friend"! A good brand name for Trafalgar Cuw's eau de Stillwell

**-san** ancient unisex suffix universal on Terasaki and Outreach, and elsewhere as well. Means "mister/sir/ms/ma'am"

**scan, full**   *n.* information, scrute, as in "Give me the full scan on Akima Mars"

**scrute**   *n.* information; see full scan (more "official" than slang)

**scut**   *n.* a derog of *sub*-ancient origin; meaning lost

**scuz**   *n.* crap, dreck, cess: undesirable person/object/situation/ news/animal

**sensies**   *n.* experiential holovision (sensavision); also expies, feelies

**sexaria**   *n.* a place devoted to sexy or sexual activity, not necessarily a husthouse 2: sexual activity involving three or more people. "Those four are having a regular sexaria in there!"

**shader**   *n. jacko* (q.v.), on planet Jorinne

**shatm**   *n.* not slang: Arabic for all naughty words and phrases

**shipdoc**   *n.* cybernetic medic: a closed cylinder into which the patient is laid, and left for treatment/cure. Shipdoc reports and sounds a signal when patient is sufficiently recovered to leave on its own feet. A rotten bedside manner, but a lot safer than hospitals

**sickofobber**   medically, a mentally ill person. Extended to derog

**sitter**   *n.* restroom, pissoir, bathroom (though not necessarily with bathing facility). One more in a long line of euphemisms.

**skink**   *n.* a truly worthless and ugly lizard, and so a derog

**slice**   *v.* to coit; n: a piece of cake (q.v.)

**slicer**   standard Galactic slang for the male sexual organ

**slime**   "Oh slime," on Jorinne, is about the same as "Oh darn/ Oh hell"

**slimeworm**   *derog,* used as "You slime" (scum, scut, shit-head, swine, etc)

**slinker shit**   *expl. very* bad cess; supershit. "What is this s-s/He's a piece of s-s"

**slipsucker**   *derog.,* as flainer, bastard, etcetcetc

**slok off**   *v.* Beat it! ("Oh, screw off.")

**slunk**   *n.* combination of slinker and hunk. Not altogether derog, then, as "stash" isn't. What Hellfire called T. Cuw when she didn't like him

**soar**   *v.* tryst; make love

**son of a Bleaker**   *derog* (mild and jocular, except to Bleaker, who'll probably reach for his knife)

**sortabounce**   *v.* what you do when you hop upward in no- or very low G and come down

**spook**   *n.* policer or secret agent; esp. bigtime policer, as TAI, TGW (see *superspook*)

**SPOSE**   *n.* Safe Point Of Subspace Entry (as opposed to jam-cram, q.v.)

**SPTC**   *n.* Safe Point for Tachyon Conversion; same as SPOSE but a more accurate term

**stash**   *n.* the vagina; 2: a female. Only denigrating to most . . . depending on circumstances and tone, of course

**stead of**   instead of/rather than: in dialog or direct thought only

**stiktite**   *n., v.* a patch on clothing to which something else is *stiktited* (as a tool, eyecorder, small container)

**Sub'nalla!**   *expl.: Subhanallah.* Ancient Arabic, serves as "Hot damn" or "Dammity"

**Sunflower**   *derog.* a Jarp-lover, to a bigot. Name of the spacer that discovered planet Jarpi

**sunsavugs**   *n.* S.O.B.s; shitheads. See *vug*

**superspook**   *n.* TGO or TGW, every time

**swine**   constantly used derog

**Tachyon Trail**   *n.* Nonexistent, for the nonexistent "subspace"—being on the Tachyon Trail is to have converted ship and crew to tachyons so as to travel faster than light (ftl)—and accelerate

**tag/play tag**   *v.* to score sexually, or attempt to. Began as professionals' term for acquiring *taps,* or johns

**Tangram**   *n.* musical group favored by Captain Jonuta and by Cleve

**Tao's doenails**   Sakyo's expletive, for alliteration (Tao is pronounced "Daow")

**tap**   *n.* a hust's john, or score

**teddy**   *derog.* ancient name for a demagogue, any demagogue

**telepresence**   *n.* see *TP*

**"Tense not, pilgrim"**   said by Taoist to self or another Taoist; stay loose and flow, in the Way

**(thumb signal)**   When a thumb is raised toward you, it signifies "OK" or "All's well"—as in the current circled index-to-thumb. "Showed her a thumb/Showed him the thumb-up sign"

**Tloo-wheetl'** *v.* fornicate, in Jarp. In Spaceways, the ' sign *as a letter* indicates a throaty aspirant or soft *k*. "'Haifa" or "ya'" are a lot easier for Galactics to pronounce than "Tloo-wheetl'"

**TP** telepresence. *Electronic* waldoes (sensory- or grip-extenders, as those presently allowing people to handle radioactive substances on the other side of shielding; or to handle sterile or contaminated substances). Telepresences provide remote access for hands, eyes—even feet/ walking.

**TP-coif** the hood of an auraprojection suit (worn as disguise while projecting a holovisual image); covers entire head without eyeholes. TP cam(era) inside coif, at eyes, provides excellent vision

**traffic-watcher** *derog.* for policer. A local nipper, usually— but might be TAI or even TGW, to an experienced dodger such as Jonuta

**Tramper Trail** standard routes for merchanters (freighter spaceships)—esp. those without expensive tachyon conversion systemry. There can be no straight-line navigation, since there's just too much debris or "debris" out there. A civserv's head may be an empty void; space is not.

**tryst** *n., v.* a date for sexual activity, extended to mean the act. "They're trysting" now clearly means that the couple is slicing.

**tune-in** *n.* the rage; the in-thing. "Leg warmers are the real tune-in these days, no matter how hideous"

**tunnelworm** *derog.* Tunnelworms exist: fat, blind, stupid, ugly-white super-slugs

**"Uh"** a conversational acknowledgment, *spoken as a word,* not grunted. Can be "Pos/Firm" or merely an "I hear you"

**unfobbied** *adj.* glued; together; having head on straight. See *fob*

**vanitize**   *v.* to enhance one's appearance, as with comb, cosmetics

**Vla!**   Jarp exclamation; not quite an expletive

**vocalock**   *n., v.* lock, as on spaceship airlock, that responds to a voiced phrase or code-word (as "Open sesame")

**vug**   *n.* (?) usually used in "What the vug was that?" Merely "vug" alone is not used, and no one has ever seen one. Pl. only in "sunsavugs/sons of vugs" (meaningless). Some think it means one of the hells; some think it means excrement (cess); no one seems sure

**wonderful**   *expl.* usually proceeded by "Oh," this is Trafalgar Cuw's Outie way of saying "Oh no!" The phrase has been picked up by some Satana Coalition members, sometimes, and by Cosi, Station Soljer Security chief (Jorinne)

**Wrig-Wri-Fla**   *n., adj.* music for a ridiculous dance (wriggle-writhe-flash)—and we've all danced to and heard various examples

**year-ess**   *n.* a year composed of twelve 30-day months of 25-hour days, used as a standard ("ess"). No one is sure why; it matches the year of no settled world along the spaceways.

**zap**   *v.* to shoot. By extension: to hit as with news

**Zap**   when capitalized: second setting on a rectaboosted or modified stopper (*q.v.*); it induces almost instantaneous unconsciousness in nearly every case within a range of a dozen meters

**zork**   *n.* low slang for penis or butt or about anything else, as in "I worked my zork off today." Maybe it's Bleaker for penis; who cares?

**zubb**   *n.* not slang; Arabic for male sexual organ